SECOND CHANCE IN BARCELONA

FIONA McARTHUR

HARLEQUIN
MEDICAL ROMANCE

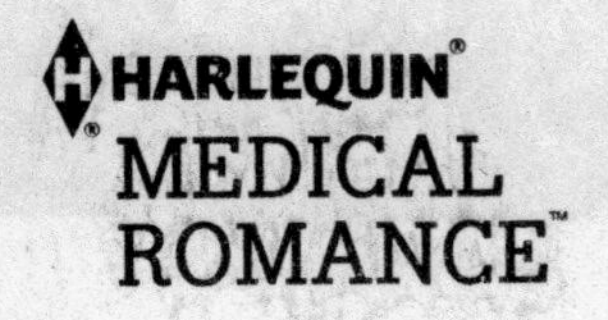

Recycling programs for this product may not exist in your area.

ISBN-13: 978-1-335-40423-7

Second Chance in Barcelona

This is a work of fiction. Names, characters, places and incidents are either the product of the author's imagination or are used fictitiously. Any resemblance to actual persons, living or dead, businesses, companies, events or locales is entirely coincidental.

This edition published by arrangement with Harlequin Books S.A.

For questions and comments about the quality of this book, please contact us at CustomerService@Harlequin.com.

Harlequin Enterprises ULC
22 Adelaide St. West, 40th Floor
Toronto, Ontario M5H 4E3, Canada
www.Harlequin.com

Printed in U.S.A.

"How is Sofia and the baby?" Felipe's voice was quiet.

"Settled. They have slept well between feeds."

"And you?"

Cleo looked up. "A couple of hours as well. Thank you. Your aircraft is comfortable and your staff very helpful. Do you sleep on flights?"

"I don't sleep much at all." Another raised brow. Again, her cheeks heated. She could attest to that.

Darn it, she just knew that when she lifted her eyes from her lap, he would be watching her with a wicked smile on his face. One that she badly wanted to wipe off. She looked up. Yep.

Instead, to both their surprise, she laughed. "Boy, this is awkward."

The tension in his shoulders seemed to fall away. "Thank you. For your honesty. You are good for me, Cleo. I try not to be so serious with you."

"Can I ask a question?"

He shrugged, the smile still playing around his lips. "I do not have to answer you, but yes."

"Why didn't you tell me who you really were and why you were here?"

"Because that was not who I was when I was with you. And it felt good."

Dear Reader,

My wonderful aunt, Maurine London, a soprano who lives in Ipswich, had her ninetieth birthday last year. After fabulous birthday celebrations, my friend Bronwyn Jameson and I traveled to Barcelona together for my first visit to Spain on the way home to Australia.

Did I hear you say you didn't know Spain was on the way home? How funny. Neither did my lovely husband realize that. He understands now. But I digress.

So of course, I wanted to write a Spanish hero, inspired by the incredible flamenco dancers we watched perform at the Villa Rosa in Madrid. And of course, my hero, Felipe, had to dance as well and amaze my Aussie midwife heroine, Cleo. Their romance starts in Australia and then they fly over to beautiful Barcelona and the fun begins.

Cleo and Felipe's journey to happiness was not an easy one, but it was worth fighting for.

I hope you enjoy Cleo and Felipe's story as they care for others before themselves.

With huge thanks to Bron, my travel buddy, and Victoria for fab editorial suggestions and Marion Lennox for being the mentor that she is.

And of course, you, dear reader—I thank you for your wonderful support.

xx *Fi*

Fiona McArthur is an Australian midwife who lives in the country and loves to dream. Writing medical romance gives Fiona the scope to write about all the wonderful aspects of romance, adventure, medicine and midwifery she feels so passionate about. When she's not catching babies, Fiona and her husband, Ian, are off to meet new people, see new places and have wonderful adventures. Drop in and say hi at Fiona's website: fionamcarthurauthor.com.

Books by Fiona McArthur

Harlequin Medical Romance

The Midwives of Lighthouse Bay

A Month to Marry the Midwife
Healed by the Midwife's Kiss
The Midwife's Secret Child

Christmas in Lyrebird Lake

Midwife's Christmas Proposal
Midwife's Mistletoe Baby

A Doctor, A Fling & A Wedding Ring
The Prince Who Charmed Her
Gold Coast Angels: Two Tiny Heartbeats
Christmas with Her Ex

Visit the Author Profile page
at Harlequin.com for more titles.

Dedicated to Marion Lennox, who has written well over a hundred wonderful books and has always been one of my huge writing heroes. I feel so blessed to have you as a friend and mentor. And someone to swim with in funny bathing hats. xx Fi

Praise for
Fiona McArthur

"I absolutely adored the story…. Highly recommended for fans of contemporary romance. I look forward to reading more of Fiona McArthur's work."

—*Goodreads* on *Healed by the Midwife's Kiss*

PROLOGUE

Wednesday, eleven p.m. Private Maternity Wing, Sydney Hospital, Australia

'SOFIA?' CLEO SPOKE quietly as she crossed to the first-time mum in the birthing unit. 'I'm Cleo Wren.'

Sofia Gonzales sat as haughty as a princess in her bed with her jet-black hair coiled in a plait on her head. Her long slender neck looked delicate against the pillows. Most telling, her elegant fingers twitched and then stiffened as she clasped them together on the coverlet with rigid tension. The girl stared unsmilingly back.

She looked fragile to Cleo. Even from that first moment she'd entered the room. So young and lost. A child, bearing a child. Alone. Cleo felt sympathy rise in her chest.

'You are the next shift?' The words were formal and surprisingly soft. The accent Spanish, her friend Jen, the previous shift's midwife, had said.

'Yes. I am. And you are Sofia?' She smiled. 'I hope we are simpatico as we will spend the next eight hours or so together until you meet your baby.'

A tiny lift of one corner of the lovely mouth. 'Jen said you are a woman of warmth, determination and strength. I need that on my side. That is simpatico enough for me.'

Despite the brisk words Cleo could see how close to breaking this young woman was and she wanted to know why. She touched her hand and Sofia's fingers closed around hers in greeting.

Sofia nodded. 'The doctor has said he will see me to deliver this baby in the morning. He thinks I will be here in labour all night.'

'You and your baby are both well and already working together. It is quite possible we can surprise him in the morning.'

'I would like that.' Labour intruded, and with the first links of connection between the two women established, something crumpled inside Sofia and she turned her face away to hide the weakness. 'I'm scared,' the girl whispered, with her soft European cadence. Sofia grabbed tighter to Cleo's hand and began to gasp through the contraction.

Cleo placed her other hand firmly on Sofia's shoulder and concentrated on transferring calmness and strength through her fingers. Young and alone. She felt so glad she'd chosen to come in here for the extra shift now. Jen had said this woman badly needed support.

Sixty seconds later, as the contraction ended, Sofia released Cleo's hand, and Cleo mimed blowing out a deep breath to demonstrate.

'Purse your lips and blow that contraction away,' she murmured as she assessed how best to help her new initiate into the wonders of birth. 'Allow your body to sink into the bed and sigh a big sigh after each contraction.'

Sofia closed her eyes and followed Cleo's instructions obediently, and when she opened them again some of the fright had receded. She blinked and already her face appeared less tightly drawn.

'There. That one is done.'

'Many more to come, though.' Sofia tried to smile. 'I'm still scared.'

Cleo nodded. 'Doing something you've never done before asks a lot of us. But I'll stay with you. By the time you've had your baby you'll have achieved one of the most amazing things in your life. You won't be scared any more. You'll have turned into a lioness to protect your young.'

'Easy for you to say.' A little haughty impatience in the tone and Cleo held in a smile. 'I'll have been in agony and it will take hours.'

'Not agony. But hours, yes, possibly. We'll work on speeding labour up. But the journey will take as long as it needs to.'

'*Sí.* The faster the better.'

Cleo glanced around the empty room. She couldn't understand the lack of support for this woman. This was a private hospital that cost bucketloads to be admitted to. Why was she alone? The previous staff had asked, and she'd just said her family were overseas. But where was the baby's dad?

'Is there anyone I can call to come to sit with you as well?'

'No.' A long pause and then quietly, 'My fiancé has left me. I am alone.'

The shock made Cleo's eyes widen. Cleo's husband had left her, too. Not as a pregnant woman in labour, thank goodness. But she understood Sofia's sadness now.

Had he left Sofia for a richer woman, more acceptable to his mother? Like hers had?

Sofia went on. 'Any family…' A pause and a definite lip curl. 'Any I would have with me are in Spain.'

So? 'I'm guessing there are family in Australia, then?'

'My cousin has destroyed my life by forcing my fiancé to leave me. He is the same as his father was. A pig.'

Well, Cleo could understand why she wouldn't want her cousin here. That was fine. She'd been thinking of female relatives or friends. 'No one else?'

'My parents are dead. Last year in a car accident.' Sofia shook her head. 'Close to me, there is just my grandmother in Spain and she is old and agreed with my cousin that he should ruin my life.' There was hurt and bewilderment as well as anger.

'You need someone here to stay with you until you give birth. May I stay until your baby has arrived?'

Sofia searched Cleo's face. 'What if my baby is not here before your shift ends?' She didn't believe her. 'Jen was here before and now she has gone.'

'Jen had already done a double shift. And she must come back tomorrow as the manager. I do these occasional shifts to stay connected to my old job when I worked here. Now I work as a retrieval nurse for patients who need a medical escort to fly home, to Australia or overseas. But I don't need to check in there again until Monday. When the new staff come on, I'll stay as a support person if your baby hasn't entered the world. I'll be here.'

'I would like that.' Sofia's eyes clung to hers. 'But why would you do this?'

Their eyes met and Cleo smiled. 'I need to be here for you at this time. Easy.' She shrugged. 'Let's check your observations and your baby's heart rate. Then, with your permission, I'll feel the position of your baby through your belly to see if it's curled itself in the best way to find a way out.'

A smile tugged on Sofia's beautiful mouth. 'Does a baby assume a position?'

Another contraction rolled over her and she moaned. Cleo held her hand through the heavy breathing and when it was done, they breathed out together.

'A position? Absolutely a baby chooses. And with the angles of your own body you can give your baby hints on slight changes that make all the difference to the length of your labour. Just by moving your centre of gravity around. We'll do that, too.'

A few minutes later the observations had been completed and found to be all within acceptable limits. 'Baby's moving down into the pelvis as expected.' They breathed through another contraction together.

Cleo sat again to chart Sofia's progress and observations on the rolling computer beside the bed. Then she saved the file and pushed the computer away.

'So now we've done that for the moment, I'll help you stand out of bed.' She pretended to frown at the bed. 'Beds are not great for healthy mums in labour because lying in bed can slow everything down.'

Sofia looked worried. 'I don't think I can move.'

'It will feel better to move, I promise. Standing adds gravity to help your baby descend even more.' She showed crossed fingers to Sofia. 'Makes labour faster!'

Sofia's eyes widened at the possibility and she rolled onto her side, suddenly eager to get up. 'Then I will stand.'

They walked around the room, pausing during the contractions, finding places of comfort before the contractions increased. The waves of labour progression were still infrequent enough for conversation.

Sofia perched gingerly on the big rubber ball when Cleo suggested it, and her eyes widened as the round softness beneath her eased her back discomfort. Together they examined the shower, and discussed the big bath in the bathroom at which Sofia looked askance.

Cleo laughed. 'You wait. If I can get you into that bath, up to your neck in warm water, I'll have trouble getting you out again. You'll love it so much.'

She rested her hand gently on Sofia's shoulder as another contraction rolled over the woman.

Sofia gripped the bathroom doorframe and forced the breath from between her lips to stay relaxed.

'Perfect,' murmured Cleo. 'You're breathing beautifully. That was a stronger contraction.'

Sofia nodded, then sagged a little when the tightness released its grip on her. 'And closer to the last one as well.'

'Which is wonderful. Stronger and closer means nearer to meeting your baby.'

Sofia raised her brows at her. 'Easy for you to say.'

'Indeed. Though in my defence I have seen this point in labour many times and women always fill me with wonder. They keep going. Like you will. Just one contraction at a time until the most amazing thing occurs and the baby is here in your arms. Keep thinking of that.'

Sofia glanced at the bed meaningfully. Cleo shook her head. 'And try to stay off the bed. Lying down slows contractions and builds tension in your body. We talked about that. More, not less discomfort.'

'I wish I could send these pains to the father of this child.' Her eyes narrowed. 'Or my horrid cousin. Yes. I would send them to *him*. He would have dragged me back to Spain before the baby was born if he could have and then I wouldn't even have had you.'

Cleo didn't like the sound of anyone being dragged anywhere against their will. Not something she had experience of. 'Can't you say no?'

'Much good that would do me. My cousin is the head of my family now. His father was my guardian and threatened me with an arranged marriage. My parents left me financially independent enough to be able to complete university in Australia. Out of his reach. I slipped away when he was ill and then he died. I was so happy living here. Now his son has ruined my life. Bah, I hate him.'

Hate. Not what they needed in labour. Cleo touched her arm. 'Then don't think about him. Tell me the most beautiful thing about your home. I've never been to Spain. I'd like to go someday.'

With effort Sofia breathed out and almost visibly shook off the strong feelings that had upset her. 'I live in Barcelona. When I was a child my mother used to take me to the Sagrada Familia. It is a beautiful church built by Gaudi on the Carrer de Mallorca.' She smiled at the memory and the tension leaked from her shoulders. 'My mother would say, "Surely this is the most beautiful church in the world." Yet it is still unfinished more than a hundred years later.'

'It sounds amazing. I must look it up. What else?'

'I love tapas. Barcelona has wonderful food.' Her voice sounded dreamy and she smiled. 'And the dancing. I love the dancing.' She was smiling now at some distant memory. 'The men are very handsome when they dance.'

Cleo smiled, relieved Sofia had calmed down. 'They sound gorgeous. Jen's boyfriend is Catalonian and he's certainly a handsome man.

They're trying to talk me into going to his night-club where there is flamenco dancing. One day I'll go.'

'Is that this Jen? From here?'

Cleo laughed. So much for privacy. No escaping it as Jen had looked after Sofia in the previous shift. 'Yes.'

Sofia smiled. 'And one of my friends told me about this hospital and Jen. So, you and I, we were destined to meet.'

Cleo thought about Jen's cry for help for this lonely young woman. 'I'd like to think so.' And then the next powerful wave stopped all discussions.

Two hours later the contractions rolled over Sofia relentlessly but, as Cleo had promised, once she'd climbed into the birth pool, the heated bathwater lapped around and supported her. As the crashing waves of transition pushed her into second stage she breathed and moaned yet remained calm.

There was a brief pause in the labour as Sofia's body prepared for the final dance of birth. Cleo anticipated what was to come as the room rested quietly with her. Soft music underlay the steady breathing of the mother. Cleo knelt beside the bath, her gloved hands resting on the edge of the bath out of the water as she waited.

The second midwife, discreetly summoned by Cleo as birth became imminent, sat unobtrusively in the corner of the room, only rising to take and record the myriad observations as required. Cleo remained focussed on Sofia as her baby's head began to descend into the world. Her charge's previous tension seemed to have been released.

When the moment of birth arrived, it was Sofia's careful hands that reached down and lifted her own tumbled underwater baby from the depths of the pool and carried her to the surface.

In support, Cleo's hands cupped the mother's hands as she broke the surface with her new daughter to rest her tiny, blue-tinged face between Sofia's breasts. Cleo wiped the baby's eyes, nose and mouth with a soft sponge and she breathed. No cry. But blinkingly awake.

Sofia's brimming eyes met Cleo's and Cleo nodded. 'Congratulations. She's beautiful. You're amazing.'

Such incredulous wonder on the mother's face. 'She's here. I did it. Thank you.'

CHAPTER ONE

Thursday

DR FELIPE ANTONIO ALCALA GONZALES, had landed in Sydney on Tuesday on his private aircraft and he'd been busy since then.

Tonight he met with Diego, another distant cousin who lived in Australia. They were heading to Diego's bar to discuss finding his cousin, Sofia, who had slipped out of sight. 'Felipe. How goes your grandmother?'

'Not well. But she is fighting her illness until I return Sofia to Spain.' Doña Luisa, the woman who had raised him when his mother had died many years ago, had asked him to retrieve his cousin, and he would do what she wished. She should not have had to ask. He would do anything for the woman who'd shown him the love he'd never received from his late father.

They'd all thought his cousin Sofia Gonzales was at university in Sydney, but instead she'd become quietly entangled with an Australian conman and was heavily pregnant by him. Diego had been watching him this last week at Felipe's request.

'Thank you, Diego. Your help has been invaluable. Though we still need to see her home to Spain before the baby is born if possible.'

'Sí.' Diego clenched his hand into a fist. 'And I would have liked to have thrashed the scoundrel, with his mistress watching, for their insults to Sofia. She is only nineteen!'

Felipe's eyes flared. 'As would I. But now their plans for her inheritance have been blocked by the family's bankers. They will get no more of her money.'

'Sofia is blaming you for running him off.'

Felipe nodded. 'Of course. She is young. Thought herself in love and she didn't believe the charges against the man.' And Felipe had used his own money to buy the conman off.

He understood Sofia's anger with him but the avarice he'd seen in the conman's eyes had quickly banished any reluctance to upset his cousin.

Sofia and her baby would be safer in Spain where his grandmother—for as long as she could—and he could watch over them. In time hopefully a suitable Catalan husband could be found for Sofia, if she was agreeable.

It should never have reached the stage that such

a leech could attach himself to his family and enthral his cousin.

He must take some of the blame for that happening, but in his defence the last year had been absolutely crazy.

His work as medical director and oncology consultant at his hospice had been all-consuming. His father's death had left him in charge of the family. Except he had failed with Sofia.

His grandmother's terminal illness had taken most of his free thoughts. That and the sudden decline of his best friend's health, too.

Sofia had been pushed aside.

Now his cousin had gone into hiding, but he knew she deserved a moment to catch her breath after the betrayal of the man she loved. He would find her and bring her home before Monday.

But the delay was driving him insane when his grandmother was fading in health back in Spain.

On Saturday Felipe strode into the Villa Rosa flamenco club in Sydney. The one you went to for the best of Spanish dancers. The one that sold the best of Catalonian wine. The one run by Diego.

Today he had tracked down and seen Sofia and her newborn baby.

Yet, when he had finally talked to his cousin, they had achieved nothing productive.

Sofia utterly refused to accompany him in his aircraft and leave Australia. Impasse. She did not believe that their grandmother was dying or that he'd promised his grandmother to bring her home.

He could give her two more nights before he had to leave for Spain. He felt as if he would explode, having been given the disquieting news that in his absence his grandmother had become more unwell, her heart failing quickly, and he needed to return.

Damn the complications created in Australia when he wanted to be in Spain and by his little grandmother's side.

Just walking into Diego's club, though, seeing the familiar trappings, hearing the familiar music and smelling the scent of fruit-filled sangria, calmed a little of his agitation.

Monday. They would leave on Monday. He had to convince Sofia that there was little time left for their grandmother.

His eyes watched the male dancer finish the eight o'clock show and Felipe admitted the man was good. Even envied him the freedom to express himself in that manner.

Felipe could dance. Frowned on by his autocratic father, it was one thing his grandmother had been firm about when his father had scorned the idea.

Even now, at thirty-six, he could remember her whispering to him not to hold his emotions inside like his father did. 'I see you when you dance.

Flamenco for you offers the release of your emotions,' she'd said.

Since then he'd incorporated many dance moves into his daily private workout routine and it soothed him. His grandmother had been amused.

Diego approached and held out his hand. 'Don Felipe.'

Felipe's anger softened momentarily at his cousin's mock deference. They had grown up together, though their lives had diverged many years ago when Diego had moved to Australia.

Diego's face saddened. 'Doña Luisa is failing, cousin?'

Felipe didn't want to talk about how much he wanted to be at home right now, but Diego knew. Had understood from the moment he'd arrived here from Spain. Instead, Felipe nodded at the Spaniard departing from the stage. 'I could stamp more than he if I let all my anger out.'

'Then why not do it?' Diego's voice was low. 'Marcos will step aside and go home early in a heartbeat to his wife. It would be good for you.' He shrugged. 'And I love to watch your passion.' A brief gesture with his hand. 'I could easily arrange for your flamenco during the last session of the evening. Perhaps enjoy the company of a beautiful woman tonight, flirt, and forget your troubles and responsibilities. I would like to see you smile before you leave.'

He didn't need the complication of a woman tonight, but to dance? Felipe's first thought of performing in the club—ridiculous. His second—he wished he could. His third—to hell with proper behaviour for his status. He'd do it. To step away from his grief, release his anger and try to go home whole on Monday.

Nobody knew him here. Perhaps his grandmother would smile when he told her.

'Do you have boots?'

At 10:00 p.m., when the time arrived for his performance, he slipped into the bar and surveyed the audience, but his gaze caught on the woman in the blue scarf and lingered. His cousin's words came back to him.

'Enjoy the company of a beautiful woman tonight and forget your troubles and responsibilities.'

She was tall and auburn-haired, with an aura of serenity that soothed his own jangling emotions, and he felt the pull of something quiet and real. Odd ramifications of her presence echoed all the way down to his waiting, angry, black-booted feet.

As he watched her, an inexplicable tendril of calm and peace entered his soul and rested there. Later, if she was still there, perhaps he would talk to her…

CHAPTER TWO

CLEO SAVOURED THE odd feeling of exhilaration in her chest and the room's aroma of perfume, spicy food and fragrant wine. The wood under her finger felt warm as she traced the etched roses on the black wooden wall beside her and followed Jen deeper into the Villa Rosa flamenco club. She glanced at her watch—what the heck? Ten at night!

Like a night shift.

The small bars and restaurants of the tiny alley on their way here had seemed filled with handsome swarthy men partnering exotic women with flashing eyes and red lips. A seething nightlife unlike any she'd seen before.

It was how she imagined across-the-world Barcelona to be, rather than a neighbourhood that lay only twenty minutes from her Coogee flat. This vibrant subculture of predominantly Spanish-speaking streets felt like another dimension.

As well as another era.

Jen's Diego, her 'Spanish hunk' in Jen's words,

owned and sang at the club they'd just entered. He'd been amused that Cleo, a flamenco-watching virgin, would see the last-minute guest dancer in the late show who by all accounts should not be missed.

And why not? Her painful divorce was finally through. A year in her new job had settled her. She needed a new direction now to find the fun she'd been missing out on. Jen was advocating the advantages of a Spanish boyfriend. Not on Cleo's menu but it was amusing to imagine.

The room sat expectantly in semi-darkness, the stage a golden finger of light bathing the guitarist as he strummed a lilting tune that caught at Cleo's throat and promised more.

A dark-haired waitress swung a jug of fruit-filled sangria onto their table without asking and poured their first drinks into heavy wineglasses before she sashayed away.

Cleo rested back in her chair and tried to believe this was Diego's place of employment.

This was totally exotic.

Cleo sipped the cinnamon-and-apple spiced wine, loosened the sky blue scarf she'd worn to keep the night chill off her shoulders outside and allowed her gaze to roam as the music picked up in tempo.

The guitar's song seeped into her skin and infiltrated her senses to beat in her veins.

A darkly dressed woman and a familiar man,

Diego, stepped onto the stage and sat each side of the guitarist. Both began to clap rhythmically, and it was Diego's lilting voice that pierced the semi-darkness as he began to sing.

Her neck prickled.

In Spanish, the lyrics held a haunting cadence that stirred Cleo's skin to gooseflesh and she turned to see Jen staring with rapt attention at her boyfriend. Yep, she'd agree with that. He was good.

Cleo's eyes drifted back to the stage, gave up trying to decipher the meaning of the words with her only fair Spanish, and allowed the pure emotion of the music to soak into her like the sweet sangria she sipped.

Both wine and music danced in her blood and made her itch to clap her hands along with the rest of the audience. Primitive feelings stirred against the calm and collected persona she projected. First came a young woman, dancing to the beat, her skirts swishing, hands flying, spinning and stamping.

Then came an older woman. The experience of living the dance vibrant in every gesture—another span of many minutes passed watching another world.

Wow, Cleo thought to herself. These performers were amazing.

Music beckoned to something she didn't understand as her foot began to tap. This whole night felt different. So fun. A crazy, completely wonderful thing to do for yesterday's birthday which had passed with only Jen to congratulate her.

'You look happy,' Jen said, beaming across at her.

'You're right,' Cleo said. 'This is fabulous.'

The room fell silent and the audience turned their heads as one to the bar.

A tall, dark-clothed man stood with his back toward the audience ten tables from the stage. When he spun unexpectedly to face them the guitar whispered a taunting note of promise to shift the mood.

In the dim light, Cleo couldn't distinguish the man's face, but the broad shoulders, strong chest and muscular arms under the black shirt were clearly defined. As were the long, muscular thighs clad in black jeans and strong calves in knee-high boots. He paused, poised, splendidly macho in silhouette.

Cleo's breath caught. The heels of his black boots glinted with gold and for a few beats of the mesmerising music he clicked them slowly where he stood.

Coal-black hair hung long and straight, shielding both sides of his face until his head lifted and he stared straight at the musicians on the stage. Commanding them. They clapped faster.

Now she could see his features and wondered if she would ever forget them again.

A hard face, full of angles and harsh planes, yet as primal and piercing as the howl of a wild animal on the full moon. Strong straight nose, sharp cheekbones and an unsmiling mouth. When he strode forward nobody spoke, they barely breathed, awed by his charisma—riveted by the respect he ruthlessly demanded.

She wasn't sure if it was the arrogant tilt of his head, the nonchalant looseness of his fingers as they swung at his sides or the slow haughty strides of his long legs as he passed, but her eyes locked on the coiled strength and beauty of his movement like everyone else's did. Then her gaze snagged on the taut backside unapologetically squeezed into those skin-tight trousers as he did a slow, languid climb of the two steps in front of them onto the stage.

Holy moly.

When this man moved there was no one else in the room.

He glanced neither left nor right, simply owned the space as he strode to the sphere of gold light that waited to focus on only him. His chin dropped, black hair fell forward, again obscuring his features, booted feet snapped together as he stood motionless, fingers rigidly splayed.

The guitar stopped with him.

Until music, and the dancer, began to glide

slowly, precisely, rhythmically perfect, gloriously arrogant. Faster the music went. Faster he spun and stamped and whirled, a story without words. Emotion soaked the air, wrapping its ethereal hand around Cleo's heart, and she had no idea why but her mouth dried as tears gathered at the corners of her eyes.

He spun and stamped, then stopped and stared haughtily over the heads of the audience, then spun again in a wild yet fluid poetry of movement that spoke without words. Called the long history of his ancestors into the hushed room.

Cleo sat captivated by the most marvellous male she'd ever seen.

This man's carved-in-stone cheekbones and arrogant chin, the way he flung his head and flashed his eyes had an aristocratic beauty that clutched at her and refused to let go.

There was something dangerously sensual that made her feel feminine and fragile and fascinated beyond reason as she stared at him, her heart thudding in time to his gold-heeled black boots.

Her teeth grazed her lip as the rate of her breathing rose with the music.

Her breath caught when he looked her way.

Who knew even hair could be erotic? Thick strands of his black-as-night locks swung and swirled and bucked as his eyes caught and held hers.

His eyes fixed on her. Then he turned away.

She puffed out a breath she hadn't realised she'd been holding.

Struggled to remember when she'd last had shameless, erotic thoughts about a man. Had she ever?

Good grief.

She forced herself to sit back and blow out the tension. Ground herself and shift the soles of her feet back and forward to feel the wooden floor beneath her shoes.

Relationships had been scarce since the divorce. She'd dived into her overseas patient retrievals, working for an agency that mainly arranged transport and medical escorts to enable ill Australians to return home. Sometimes overseas visitors required medical supervision as well to return to their homelands. It was demanding but interesting work. Sometimes she was out of the country for a week or more at a time. Then there was the occasional labour ward shift work with Jen.

That had been enough to curtail her social life. No time for dalliance. Let alone sex.

The only males she saw were clients or doctors—and she'd learned her lesson about doctors. She'd just divorced one after all. None were men she'd think about in that way.

This way.

At least at this moment—with this man.

Her mind imagined his sexy mouth on hers.

Oh, my, she thought as her eyes clung like his clothes to his body. She almost laughed out loud.

A fierce cape-swirling matador who moved like liquid added heat-stoking dance gestures that reached into her soul and from across the room cupped her face with a look when he stopped.

When he snapped his heels together and focussed on her it was as if he circled her body with a wicked swirl of his large elegant hand and brushed her skin.

The last thing she'd thought she'd feel tonight was heated thighs but right now she needed to shift in her seat and squeeze her knees together.

He was looking at her.

Again.

Often.

Now almost all the time. Whenever his head came back her way his eyes were on hers.

As if speaking with his dance. Coal-black eyes bored into Cleo's through the rhythmic music and flowing movement. Her hand crept to her chest.

And always his eyes would clash and command her not to look away.

She couldn't.

The way he twirled and twisted and suddenly stopped hypnotised her like a timid creature trapped in blinding headlights.

When he finished, arms out, complete, as the music died, Cleo's pulse rate had risen to somewhere akin to a medical emergency.

The lights went on and applause and adoration rose like a tornado into the high roof. Then it finally died down as a surge of people swarmed him.

Cleo sat back and let out a long shuddering breath.

Surreptitiously she watched him speak to his adoring fans, raise his hand, bow briefly, then bend his head to speak to Diego, before striding away without looking in her direction.

Her heart thudded and her skin tingled with an afterglow of excitement, definite arousal and a strange, hollow, spreading disappointment.

Let down. Deserted. Stupid.

What had she been thinking? That he'd come see her? He'd been an entertainer and she had certainly been entertained. Aroused, in fact. Had she expected him to come across and chat?

And yet, out of the darkness and across the wooden floor to their table, the dancer strode her way. His heated body suddenly loomed beside her and he leaned close, the scent of steaming male and some amazing masculine cologne mixed, the sensual aroma heady. His eyes captured hers, dark and dangerous, as he held out a large elegant hand.

'I am Felipe.'

CHAPTER THREE

FELIPE APPROACHED THE table where the woman with the blue scarf and Diego's Jen were sitting and he knew this was a bad idea. What was wrong with him?

His return to Spain on Monday had been arranged and yet the moment he'd seen this woman—felt this woman—she'd cast her net over him like that powerful woman in history. Diego had said, when he'd asked his cousin at the end of the dance, that her name was Cleo. Fitting. Cleopatra. Queen.

He wanted her. And couldn't have her. He knew that. He'd never been a believer in casual sex. But perhaps a little post-dance distraction would be acceptable. For that was all it could be—if it could even be that. He would talk to her. Find something to banish the fascination that pulled him to her.

Already he'd done something frowned upon for his station. To bare his soul in a public performance, let loose his anger and sadness, and find the hope that the dance always gave him since he'd first learned the moves. The dance allowed him to shed who he was, his responsibilities, the emotions of the last days, and yet all through that dance, every turn, he'd seen her.

Been drawn to her.

Danced for her.

Something in her eyes grabbed his chest and squeezed and he was aware that throughout the dance he'd shared that connection with her.

So here he was.

Standing beside her in the bright lights of post-performance with his hand out.

When she put her fingers into his he carried them to his lips and breathed in her scent… He closed his eyes to savour her and smiled at the small tremor he felt go through his mouth from her skin. Opened eyes again to catch her gaze and kiss her wrist.

Her hand caught warm and precious in his. Destined. Which was ridiculous.

Clear, cool sapphire-blue eyes, fine features and a determined chin… There was nothing classically beautiful but he found her face utterly arresting. Compelling. Incredibly fascinating. Her brows rose at his intimate salute.

Not so amusing was his sudden aching thirst for more than that small taste of her. To wrap himself around her and breathe her in as if she could fill his lungs with life.

'Diego says your name is Cleo. Like Cleopatra.' He lifted out the chair next to hers. 'Will you allow me to share a drink with you?' He did not give her his family name. This could go nowhere, after all.

Diego lifted his hand in acknowledgement and smiled, and then walked around the table to Jen, whose eyes were fixed on his cousin.

Felipe signalled to the waitress who had appeared with the bottle of sparkling wine he'd ordered and four empty glasses on a tray.

She put them down and opened it beside them. He indicated the bottle. 'This is Lonia Cava, from Catalonia. It tastes of white peach, melon and apple.' His eyes met Cleo's. 'I believe it is your birthday?'

He watched her eyes widen, enough to see the gold amidst the brilliant blue of her irises and then the irises expand enough for him to fall in even further. Her blue gaze seemed bottomless.

'It was. Yesterday,' she said, her voice low and pleasing. What was it about this woman that made him dream of foolishness he shouldn't even contemplate? And with a woman from the same country as Sofia's conman?

If he wasn't careful, this would end with piercing sweetness and an unfamiliar longing on his empty flight home.

CHAPTER FOUR

CLEO STRUGGLED WITH his presence, so large and almost vibrating with heat and sex and all the images in her brain from the dance. But she tried very hard not to show it.

The music started again in the background, taped this time, and after a brief acknowledgement of the newcomer and some compliments on his dance, Diego and Jen became engrossed in their own conversation.

She was left alone with the dancer. 'Thank you for the wine.'

But under the table her hand still tingled. Just that feel of this man's lips on her wrist had made her belly kick. Which was ridiculous. She was thirty. No virgin.

She'd been married and divorced, for goodness' sake. But what she'd felt for Mark had been slow to grow and stupid in hindsight and she wouldn't do that again. On her side anyway, it had been nothing like this instant, searing awareness and aching need for him to pull her closer.

This was raw. Crazy. Pulsing with the promise of experiencing something way out of her normal world and she wondered what she'd done to draw someone like him to her. But he was here now.

There was that temptation to be mad. A magnetic pull to do something out of character for once. To consider whether she could pretend she knew the rules of the game. To feel captured and appreciated and not feel discarded afterwards.

She didn't know where it could go. Or even if it should go anywhere. 'Are you in Australia long?' It was the least she could ask.

'I leave on Monday.'

She allowed her eyelids to close as she considered that. Two days and he would be gone. Opened her eyes and nodded. 'That's too bad.' Or maybe not.

She glanced at her watch. Eleven o'clock. Not yet the witching hour but she was under some kind of spell that she didn't want to wake from. Something with no future.

She took a sip of her wine and it sparkled and fizzed on her tongue, light and delicious, and divine. Like him. 'Thank you for the wine.' She lifted her glass to him. 'And the birthday wishes. I'll just have this but then I'll have to go.'

He bent his head in her direction, apparently content with her answer, and she thought with a flicker of disappointment that he could've asked her to please stay.

His fingers waved to the door. 'It is warm. I wish to be outside. Would you like to walk from here? Along the street? Away from this room?'

And suddenly she knew she would like that. Very much. Just a walk. She wasn't planning on more, especially with a sexy Spaniard leaving on Monday, not for one night. But she did want to get out of there and spend a few moments with the man opposite and fizz and bubble like the wine and be daring.

Before she went home.

To be alone.

'I could walk with you. For a few minutes.' Whoa. And she'd actually said it. Sometimes she surprised herself.

Jen looked up, as did Diego, and they both nodded. 'I vouch that he is a gentleman,' Diego said, and grinned that sexy, sunbeam smile that had won her friend. Then added more teasingly, 'Unless you wish otherwise.'

'A walk.' Felipe drained his glass and stood. 'A fine idea. Shall we go?'

Who said, 'A fine idea'? This sexy Spanish guy apparently. Well, then, she felt like doing something unlike Cleo Wren. Not her usual cautious behaviour.

She drank the last contents of her own glass,

and the pale magic wine tingled and bubbled and made her smile as she reached for her bag.

Out on the street the alley seemed alive with laughter and the chink of glasses and the glow from streetlamps and pseudo Spanish *cantinas*. Far too alive and alert for nearly midnight in her usual world. 'Don't these people ever sleep?'

'Siesta allows the use of the night.' He took her hand. The fun came back with the rush and sizzle of a firecracker ready to explode as his fingers wrapped confidently around hers.

Her face turned up to his. 'Tell me about Spain. Where do you live?'

The dark skin around his eyes crinkled. 'Barcelona. The most beautiful city in the world.'

She tossed a smile up at him. 'How funny. I live in Sydney.' She spread her free hand in an arc in front of her. 'The most beautiful city in the world.'

He laughed and she grinned at the pleasure it gave her to see him relax. He'd seemed so self-contained and serious as he'd danced, and when he'd first come to the table as well. This outside man was easier to walk with.

Their hands swung lightly between them, entwined, warm, and she glanced down, surprised how easy she felt holding hands with a stranger. She shook her fingers. 'And why does this feel so relaxed when I don't know you at all?'

He tilted his head at her. 'You forget. We met

through the dance. I saw you. It is magic when that happens.'

'Have you been dancing long?' Did he do it for a living, like Diego sang? Did he own a similar club in Barcelona? All questions she wanted to ask but she bided her time. Impatience didn't fit in with this night.

He looked away from her. Pensively. 'I have danced all my life.'

She remembered his passion and power. 'You're very good.'

He turned to look down at her and laughed at that. 'No. I am not very good. I am brilliant.'

She shook her head at his boasting but his confidence delighted her. 'Really?' She arched her brows at him. 'You're certainly not shy.'

This raised his brows. 'Do you know many Spanish men?'

She did have limited experience of the Spanish. 'I know Diego.'

'Diego is a good man. But he, also…' another amused smile '…is not shy.'

She could vouch for that. But to Jen he was kind and funny as well.

They'd walked from the alley now and onto the footpath that led to Coogee, away in the distance, past two- and three-storey houses that had glimpses of the ocean from their top balconies. Their hands still swung between them. Cars zoomed past, sweeping them with more light than that cast by the streetlamps, but the number of vehicles was slowing as the night progressed.

Each time he was illuminated she admired his presence more.

Maybe he would be back in Australia someday. 'How do you know Diego?'

'From Barcelona.'

He asked another question, instead of offering more information about himself. 'Do you live near the beach?'

'I do.' Two could play at minimal answers.

His brows went up as if aware she was retaliating in kind. 'And does anyone else live with you?'

And why would you want to know that? But she didn't say it. 'I could tell you,' she agreed, 'but then I'd have to kill you.'

He laughed. 'I like you, Cleopatra.'

Lord, she was sick of that name. 'Cleo, please. Nobody calls me Cleopatra.'

'Your mother did.' He bumped her with his shoulder. Something fun and silly and she bumped him back. As if they'd known each other for many years, not just minutes.

'True. But she was heavily into the queens of Egypt during her pregnancy. I suppose I should be glad I wasn't called Hatshepsut.'

He laughed again and she didn't know why she felt so pleased every time he did. With every chuckle a little more tension seemed to ease from his broad shoulders and his face softened. 'I like the sound of your mother,' he said.

She would have liked you as well. Or fallen for your looks at least. 'I wish I could tell her that.'

His face turned sad and she looked up at him, brows drawn, but he went on. 'I'm sorry. My mother, too, is gone. But we are adults. Is there a husband for Cleopatra?'

A roundabout way to ask. She enjoyed his odd use of English. 'There was a husband. A very conceited man. He is gone now, figuratively and legally.'

He squeezed her hand. 'My condolences. And to clarify, I am not conceited at all. Do not be concerned that I know all. I can dance. But I cannot paint or sing or write a great novel.'

'Do you have a wife?'

He laughed. 'No. Much to my grandmother's despair. There is nobody who would complain that I walk a beautiful woman home in the dark.'

It had been a long time since a handsome man had called her a beautiful woman. 'Thank you for the compliment.' She didn't believe him but it was nice to pretend. She'd needed this. 'Are you walking me home? I thought we were just walking down the hill.' Her cheeks felt hot.

He looked down at her and his eyes had warmed. 'Your husband was a fool.' Said very softly.

'Let's not discuss him.' Talk about a mood-breaker.

He snapped his fingers. 'Easily.'

She laughed. He had an unexpected humour. 'Have you been in Sydney long?'

'Four days.'

And two more until he flew out again. 'Six days seems barely enough to get over the flight.' She knew about rapid long-distance flights. 'Was there a reason for such a rushed visit?'

He looked at her and his gaze shifted away to the bottom of the hill where the sounds of the ocean were beginning to whisper to them as they drew closer. 'Yes.'

She felt the wall as a cool breeze between them. The harsh-faced man she'd first seen was back. His reasons were not for her information. She didn't know this man. What was she doing here, alone with him?

She stopped walking. Looked ahead to the lights of her unit, now in sight. Did he need to know where she lived?

'I can walk from here. Thank you.'

He closed his eyes and shook his head. Gave a crooked, apologetic smile. 'I'm sorry. I am not the open, sharing person I begin to think you are. To say what I think out loud is hard for me. Unlike you.'

'That's a sweeping statement, Felipe.' She saw

something flit across his face, a bitterness, as he compressed his lips.

She decided. 'But, still, perhaps it is better if I go on alone.'

She searched his face in the gold light of the streetlamp and something in his eyes made her sad. 'It was very nice to meet you.' She reached up and very gently put her lips against his. 'Good-bye, Felipe.'

Felipe inhaled the scent of her, savoured the feather-light touch of her lips on his, and pulled her closer for a moment in time. She was right. He should let her go.

Yet he reached forward with his mouth softening, gently exploring, waiting for her to pull back.

When she remained compliant, he slid his hand around her neck and pulled her snugly against him. Gently brushed her lips with his own, back and forth, and to his satisfaction she opened to him like a flower and he explored the wonder that was Cleo.

Her taste and scent and softness warmed parts of him that had been cold for too long. Her hand, between their chests, squeezed tighter around his and he pulled her more firmly against his heart.

After many long, long moments that held the breath of time in the darkness on a footpath near the bottom of the hill, they stepped back and searched each other's faces—seeing the answer to a question that hadn't been spoken out loud.

Still her hand was held warmly and softly and they smiled at each other. 'Or I could come a little further with you?'

He slipped his hand further up her wrist to feel her pulse pounding beneath his fingers and she nodded.

A few minutes later she stopped at a door. Or at least an entry to a block of units.

In the distance he could hear the pound of crashing waves quite loudly and even taste the tang of salt, but close to her he could mostly smell the enticing scent of Cleo and feel the warmth of her skin brushing against his.

She lifted keys from her handbag and opened the bottom entry door, turning back to face him. She searched his face and something, he didn't know what it was, that she saw made her relax. 'Would you like to come in?'

'Very much,' he said softly, ignoring the voice of reason in his head that told him to move away. Step back. He could not.

He followed her straight back and charmingly rounded bottom up the stairs, admired her long, slim legs and the way her hips moved as she climbed one flight and then a second. Tension coiled inside him, his attraction to her expanding like a chemical reaction, and by the time they reached her door his heart pounded from proximity to and promise from this mesmerising woman.

She glanced back at him as she turned the key in the lock, but she didn't hesitate to push open the door.

When she moved inside, he followed. Reached back with a steady hand and removed the keys she'd left dangling, then pushed the door shut behind them with a gentle click.

To the left in the dimly lit room lay a small table and he dropped the keys on his way to reach for her.

'This is crazy,' she whispered.

'Is there something wrong with crazy between two consenting adults?'

She sighed but curled her fingers into his shirt and tugged him closer. 'No. Now is good. You'll be gone soon.'

'We have tonight. And I am prepared,' he patted his pocket, 'to keep you safe.'

He saw in her eyes that she chose to accept him and she relaxed against his chest. They kissed. His hands slid reverently over her soft breast and slid the blue scarf from her shoulders to kiss her beautiful neck.

Tomorrow he would think about Monday and going home.

CHAPTER FIVE

CLEO FELT THE slide of silk from her neck as this tall, muscular stranger kissed her skin. Heat flooded her. She should be feeling nervous, or wary, or guilty, but the emotions most prominent were excitement and arousal, and possibly impatience.

'Beautiful,' he murmured against her skin. *'Bella.'* When she looked into his eyes they were almost black, yet warm, and totally focussed on her with a wonder she didn't expect.

When he'd kissed her before, on the street, it was as if she'd tasted the man within and trusted him without reason but with complete faith. She saw that again now. As if she recognised his moral ground as one she, too, could live with. She'd seen her own need to be someone else for the night reflected in his eyes. What was it about their connection that had brought them to this point so fast and with such a sureness that what they shared would be right? Later, perhaps, she would find the answer. If there was time. But they had all night.

'Your home is like you,' he said quietly as he stood holding her shoulders. 'Calm, welcoming and filled with a serenity that makes me want to learn how to be in your space.' His big hands ran warmly and possessively over her, stroking the skin of her arms and her shoulders as if every slide felt wonderful to him.

His hands felt just as amazing on her.

'You're in my space now,' she said softly. Reaching up and putting her hand flat on the iron of his chest above his pectorals. Pushing a little as she marvelled at the wall of muscle. Smiling at his understated strength.

'Thank you.'

'You should. I can't think of another man who has been in here since I bought the place.'

His eyes crinkled at that and he nodded in appreciation. 'I am blessed then.' He bent his head and with one hand cupping her cheek he leaned in and kissed her. His mouth gentle, then more firm as she pushed into his body to press closer. 'Do not plan on much sleep tonight.'

Her heart rate sped. Her belly kicked and the sensual woman inside her that had been hiding all these years smiled like a cat and stretched.

This man could kiss like there was no tomorrow.

She lifted curved hands to slide them around

his neck to pull him into her. His tongue touched hers, dipped and teased, and she gasped at the spike of fierce, throbbing heat in her belly as his mouth seduced her.

And still they stood fully clothed! Somewhere, distantly, with the rest of her indistinct thoughts, she wondered at his patience.

Her previous experience had not included extended dalliance before the deed, and this was driving her crazy.

As if he knew, he chuckled and lifted her until her toes left the ground. She was no small woman but he was a dancer, no doubt used to twirling compliant females in his arms.

She looked down at him as he held her up and her surprise delighted him.

'This is the first time any man has twirled me,' she whispered in his ear.

'You are a woman who deserves special treatment. I wish I could teach you to dance with me. But there are other things we might do instead.' He smiled a man's smile and pulled her hips in towards him and cupped her bottom, so she wrapped her legs around him and savoured being wanton and wild.

Was this her?

He must have decided which was her bedroom, because he backed her towards it, his mouth kinked, watching her eyes, occasionally glancing ahead to keep them safe until she felt the end of her bed behind her legs.

Very, very slowly, as if to prove he had all the time in the world, he lowered her the length of his hard body until her feet touched the ground. They stood there for a moment pressed breast to chest.

Heat and need and urgency on her side, tenderness, heat and patience on his. Slowly he turned her body, slid the zipper from the top of her neck to the waist of her dress and slid one shoulder off.

She closed her eyes as his warm lips trailed along her skin. Then he pushed the other shoulder off and repeated the gesture. Her knees trembled.

He turned her back to face him and kissed her mouth as if her lips were petals he did not wish to crush and she felt the sting of emotional tears that didn't fall.

Then his fingers caught in her now rucked bodice, stroked the valley between her breasts and hooked the dress to slide it with a rustle into a colourful puddle at her feet.

'You are beautiful. Magnificent.' His voice low and reverent, and she lifted her chin. Suddenly not shy. She reached for him.

Now their movements quickened, both working the clothes from the other's body until two naked lovers lay skin to skin with strips of light through the window painting them in patches, light that shifted and rolled with them slowly into the night.

They rose and went into the shower together, soaping each other, murmuring in approval and amusement and desire.

At three they ate hot buttered raisin toast and drank tea, and he spoke of his father, a hard man who had sent him away when his mother had died. And the grandmother whom he loved, who was dying. 'My father told me to be a man and not hinder the family with emotions, and so I tried to avoid showing my feelings to others.'

'You can show me,' she said very quietly.

He smiled. 'You and my grandmother, because she would have none of it either. When I first went to her, a small boy of seven, grieving my mother silently, she demanded I not keep my thoughts to myself. She pushed me to learn the dance. From that time she has been the only person I allow to question my deeper thoughts.'

'She encouraged your dancing?'

'Despite my father.' He smiled at that. 'The dance allows me peace. She has given me so much that I cannot repay.'

She felt her heart ache with the loss she could see he was already dreading.

'Who will care for her when she is nearing the end?'

He lifted his head. Suddenly fierce. 'Me. Though there is a hospice in Barcelona, newly finished, designed for peace and tranquillity.' She could see he was thinking of it.

'A good place. Similar to the feeling I get in your home.' And she felt the warmth of his approval as a glow. But his eyes were far away. 'But enough of my sadness. Tell me of your parents.'

She told him of when they'd died in a boating accident in the harbour. Four years ago. How she'd been lost by being suddenly orphaned, and of the man who had said he loved her, had promised to honour and cherish her for ever, and yet had cheated on her and then discarded her. How she'd left her chosen profession to escape the toxic memories and start afresh.

They talked of Coogee, and Barcelona.

With his immersion in her, his concentrated attention, something shifted in her. Something had begun to heal from being torn. Mended by his wonder of her. Reminding her she was a woman this man wanted.

He fed her the last scrap of toast and carried her laughing back to bed. With renewed energy.

But not once did they talk of the morning, or the next day after that when he would be gone, and she accepted that.

At sunrise he dressed, kissed her deeply, and without further words between them he left. She was sad, disappointed, but didn't regret the night. Couldn't.

And she slept most of the day.

On Monday morning the salty breeze from Sydney Harbour pushed Cleo faster than she intended through the revolving door of the Medical Assistance Travel Escorts (MATE) offices. She liked providing safe and calm transport for those unwell and stranded. She stood breathless and disorientated after the revolution spat her out into the lobby.

Not like her usual composed self at all.

But then nothing had been the same since the early hours of Sunday morning. In fact, her lips still felt swollen and every now and then she'd find herself smiling. Wickedly.

But today was all about work. Monday had started strange and had become increasingly odd.

Apart from the fact that today was the day Felipe was leaving. He'd told her that. And that was a good thing. She would soon stop looking to see if he was below her window again. They'd had one incredible night, which was safer, in fact, than giving your vulnerable heart away for a husband's betrayal. No wife should ever see another woman in her husband's bed.

This way there could be no betrayal, but if Felipe hadn't been leaving, then perhaps she would have asked Jen what she knew about him.

But he was leaving.

Maybe one day Felipe would be back.

Today her list of errands had taken less time than expected to complete. She always ran errands before she left on a job. This one had only just come through and she knew little about it yet. But the destination excited her beyond all reason. Barcelona. Spain must have been in her stars this month.

And today fate had smiled on her to make this morning easy. Every parking spot had appeared where she'd never seen an empty space before.

Every traffic light turned green instead of red.

And once she was parked in a prime, unmetered position, the wind had seemed to propel her here at twice the rate she would normally have walked.

All errands had been done and she was still early.

At the oak reception desk Angie Peck, pay clerk, crisis manager and unflappable international flight and transport co-ordinator, swung her brown fringe towards the new arrival and smiled.

'Look what the wind blew in. Morning, Cleo.' Angie's chocolate-brown eyes twinkled infectiously. 'Turbulent out there? What's the word for that Spanish wind?'

Cleo thought for a moment. 'No idea.' She'd been listening to her Spanish language lessons all day yesterday as she'd stared dreamily out to sea from her bedroom window. She'd wanted to learn the meaning of some of the words that her handsome dancer had whispered to her. Felipe. She didn't know his last name. But then he didn't know hers either. It had been a fleeting but fierce one-night stand and had left her feeling unsettled but glowing. Still couldn't believe that wanton woman had been her.

Angie tapped her forehead. 'I've got it, the levanter. Well, we have a small wind of change in store for you this morning, too. On your mode of transport.'

Cleo raised her brows. 'Any chance you'll tell me what it is?'

'All will be revealed inside.' Angie gave a dramatic wave at the entry to the inner sanctum. The door of the MATE inner sanctum stood shut. Odd.

The receptionist added cryptically, 'Your special calming skills will be appreciated. His nibs is already worked up.'

With a last puzzled glance at Angie, Cleo knocked firmly on the panelled fascia and waited.

She'd completed almost two dozen overseas transfers of pregnant women or new mums and their babies since she'd come to work for MATE nearly a year ago. She'd also accompanied many general patients who had been sick or injured, clients of all ages, but as the agency's star midwife she'd never been called to the office to discuss a case prior to transfer. It had always been an email or a phone call then meet the client at the hospital.

In the case of midwifery assignments, it was usual for her to meet them at the private wing of the Sydney hospital where the rich and famous went to give birth. Like Sofia had. She wondered how the young mum was getting on. Cleo hadn't seen Jen since Saturday.

She'd thought all of the MATE clients were VIPs. It wasn't cheap to hire a midwife to travel with you, so what made this assignment so special that a face-to-face meeting was needed?

After a moment the door swung open and the tall, spare figure of Sir Reginald with his silver-grey temples and Savile Row grey suit stood back to invite her in. 'Ah, Cleo, thank you for coming.'

Sir Reginald gestured her to the seat in front of his desk, though he didn't sit down.

He paced.

That, too, was odd.

'Don Felipe Alcala Gonzales is our client.'

Amazing how many Felipes there were from Spain. The shop assistant this morning in the post office had been Felipe. And the pizza guy who'd delivered to her on Sunday night had worn a shirt with 'Felipe' on it. She'd read his name and had had to stop staring at it.

A bit like buying a red car of a certain make. You saw them everywhere after that.

Her brief liaison with her own Felipe was done. A bit of a hard act to follow despite the fact he'd kissed her goodbye and left without a word.

Best not go there. Too recent not to blush about.

Her boss went on. 'Don Felipe is the cousin of Sofia.'

'Gonzales.' Recognition flared in her brain. 'Sofia, as in the woman I looked after in labour on Wednesday night?'

'Yes. She specifically asked for you. She'd like you to escort her and her baby home to Barcelona and her cousin is the man paying the bills. He is the *cabeza de la família*—the head of the Gonzales family—and one of the richest families in Barcelona.'

Cleo's eyes widened. They were VIPs indeed. And still Sofia had been alone in labour?

Cleo felt glad she was escorting Sofia and not the cousin if this was what he did to the normally composed Sir Reginald. She remembered Sofia using the word 'hate'.

'Don Felipe has decided to oversee all the arrangements himself and accompany you on your flight.' Sir Reginald's words dropped into the silence between them.

Sofia would not be happy about that. She inclined her head. Hopefully she wouldn't have to see much of Sofia's ogre.

Sir Reginald fidgeted, back behind his desk now as she sat down, and if she wasn't mistaken, the usual unflappable head of the agency looked strangely nervous. 'I fear your client is very much unhappy with the Don. And now he has convinced her to go, he wishes to ensure she arrives safely in Spain. Thus, he insists on being present as well.'

'You're warning me there will be tension between them during the flight?' Why would that be a warning Sir Reginald felt he needed to give her? 'I thought my job is to ensure Sofia and her baby arrive in good health?' Cleo's comment hung in the air between them as a question. Did this Don want to micromanage Sofia? Or her?

She turned to Sir Reginald and said carefully, 'What arrangements are planned for our transfer?'

The aristocratic fingers shuffled desk papers again. 'You will be flying in Don Felipe's private aircraft.'

She didn't much like the idea of being totally under the control of anyone apart from the captain flying the plane.

Especially this Don Felipe, who agitated her boss. And her client.

She sat back and folded her hands in her lap. Sir Reginald was always a reasonable person. 'Are you sure my presence is necessary, then?'

'Yes. It is. Sofia has only consented to return to Spain with him if she has you as her companion.'

Sofia was calling the shots, then? Their rapport had been strong in labour. And she would be delighted to accompany the young mum. Then she remembered. 'I did mention to her this is what I usually do. She must have thought about it later.'

'Sofia has decided that nobody else will do for the flight over and has requested you as her confidante for the first two weeks postnatally when you arrive, if you will agree to stay on.'

Jen would be thrilled about this. She'd wanted Cleo to fly to Barcelona with her for a year now. Ever since she'd started dating Diego.

No doubt she'd be even more adamant since Saturday night. But Cleo doubted she'd find one male dancer amongst the five point five million people who lived in Barcelona. Even she wasn't that optimistic.

Then the rest sank in. 'Two weeks?' Cleo raised questioning brows at Sir Reginald. 'It's not unusual to stay an extra day or two but two weeks seems excessive, surely?'

Sir Reginald shuffled his disarrayed papers and avoided her eyes. 'It all changed today. By the express orders of Don Felipe. And the reason Don Felipe asked me to arrange this with you. Your final say pending, of course.'

'Just how reluctant is Sofia to return to Spain?'

Her boss grimaced. 'Very.'

Reluctance was one thing, but Cleo hoped Sofia wasn't being forced in any way by her cousin. She tried another tack. 'And the baby's father? Does he have a say in this?'

'Apparently he is no longer…' a pause '…in the picture.'

Well, she'd known that already. Sofia had told her. But she wondered if his permission had needed to be sought. She'd seen Spanish determination at first hand. Her Spanish lover had left without a forwarding address after one of the most incredible nights of her life. Still, she had no regrets.

Back to work. Not her problem. Any of the legalities could be handled by this Don.

'I hope the father of the child knows the baby is going.'

The barest hint of amusement crossed Sir Reginald's face. 'I believe so.'

Well, that was good news at least. But this was becoming clouded with what had happened to her on Saturday night and she needed to stop that. Think clearly. Probably because the ogre cousin's name was Felipe, too.

She shook her disquiet off. She needed to remain professional.

'I think I should chat to Sofia first. Just check about the two weeks. That it's really her idea and not her bossy cousin's.' Her voice remained calm and quiet, the gentle epitome of reasonableness despite her instinct screaming there was something off here.

Sir Reginald straightened and his gaze sharpened. 'You're thinking of declining the assignment?'

She looked at her boss. 'No. But there are many things to consider. The fact Sofia has agreed to go at all. The private flight, supervised by the Don. The length of time. Two weeks together with Sofia under the control of an unknown despot? Sofia and I do need to talk about this first.'

'I don't think he's a despot.' Sir Reg looked amused.

'That's not what Sofia said.' Did the young mum really want her or was everyone pushing them together? Unease grew but her sympathy for the newly single Sofia rose another notch at all these men deciding her future for her.

She glanced at her boss, who had an odd gleam in his eye. 'Are you happy to arrange that, Sir Reginald?'

'Of course. I think a meeting is an excellent idea considering the length of time and the personalities involved. I'll have Angie sort that out for this morning, as soon as possible.'

Cleo nodded.

'You can discuss the departure time after your visit,' Sir Reg said quietly, as if to himself.

Obviously, he was keen for her to go. She wondered if there was a large bonus at stake here, as well as the usual exorbitant fee charged by the agency.

The older gentleman rose.

'Thank you for the extra information.'

CHAPTER SIX

TWO HOURS LATER Cleo pulled a hospital chair closer to the bassinet beside the bed. Studied the sleeping baby. Leaned nearer to peer in and saw the name, which was new to Cleo. Isabella.

'Congratulations again. Isabella is a lovely name. She's even more beautiful than when she was born.' The genuine warmth in Cleo's voice brought the young mother's smile back to her eyes.

Sofia's worried face softened as she looked at the sleeping baby. 'She is like a doll. Babies are so perfect when they sleep.'

Cleo's mouth tilted into a smile. 'How is she when she's awake?'

'Noisy. Petulant if I'm too slow feeding her.' A soft sigh and suddenly the young woman looked like any besotted mother. Vulnerable, protective, anxious to do the right thing by her child. 'Such big eyes watch me as she drinks and I fall more in love with her every minute.'

Cleo knew she would help Sofia despite this

Don Felipe, who made even her boss nervous. 'My employer mentioned you would like me to stay for two weeks as you settle back in Spain? Is that what you want? Some assistance in the postnatal period?'

Sofia huffed out a breath. 'He says my grandmother is very unwell. I do not really believe him, but I have decided I must return in case there is some truth in this. But I will not be bullied by Felipe. I hate his interference.'

This man certainly stirred a reaction. 'Hate's a strong sentiment to have when your baby is nearby.' As if to highlight her words the baby in the crib twisted her face and let out a mewl of distress.

Instinctively, Sofia's hand went out to smooth the covers in a gentle caress. 'Can she feel my emotions?'

'Of course. You are the most important person in the world to her. Naturally she is attuned to you.'

'I forget you are one of these new age midwives.'

Cleo laughed. 'I believe we create our own destinies if that's what you mean. And most of us can feel other people's emotions. If you want me to accompany you, then for the moment I'd like to help you create a relaxed aura when you carry your baby back to Spain. Babies respond to their mother being calm.'

She smiled again. 'And we are to travel the easy way in a private aircraft. Is it so bad to be transported in comfort, with others dealing with all the arrangements?'

'No. I have accepted that. It's Felipe I object to.'

Yet that very assurance wavered with uncertainty and Cleo's heart went out to this woman dealing with her world in turmoil. What sort of man was this older, aristocratic, interfering Felipe of Sofia's? She couldn't imagine that scenario. How did one bribe a loving fiancé away from someone? And if it happened, where did that leave Sofia? How hard would it be to be a calm mother when your world had been destroyed?

It was hard enough having a first baby when everything was smooth sailing—let alone being a single parent under someone else's authority with betrayal all around.

Sofia must be feeling she had no allies.

Well, she had *her*.

Though a voice at the back of Cleo's mind wondered if Isabella's father could be bought off so easily, then how much of a loss was he? Perhaps a man like her own not-so-dear departed ex? But that would be presuming too much.

'Well, for the next few days try to think of Don Felipe as a means to an end. Like a contraction in labour. Painful but necessary to get us safely to Spain.'

Sofia's face tightened and then she morphed into a cascade of breathy giggles that surprised them both. 'Oh…' she wiped her eyes '… I'm so glad you were there when I had my baby.'

'Me, too.' Yes, she did miss being with women at birth. It wasn't often she had time to roster in a birthing suite shift. But she loved her job now as well. Helping people find strength when they were vulnerable, support when they were desperate and safety when they felt at risk away from home. She was really enjoying the different-aged clients now, too. Especially the elderly and frail.

Those accomplishments made her work a real pleasure, and the daily change of assignments had focussed her in redirecting her thoughts very nicely from the past.

'I think the next two weeks will be easier as your bond with Isabella grows. Already I can see how wonderful you are together, and I think I can help.'

'I need someone strong on my side.' Sofia's eyes narrowed. 'Especially if I have to spend any time with *him*.' She glanced at the elegant watch on her wrist. 'He is coming to see me in two hours.'

Yes. Cleo would accompany this young woman and stand by her side for the next two weeks. And if her nemesis was coming soon they'd better get started.

Travel escorts made travelling easy for their

clients. Cleo gained much of her job satisfaction in safely escorting frail or delicate clients back to their loving families, either domestic or overseas, regardless of the trickiness of the situation.

She was good at it.

Resourceful, calm, efficient and friendly with impressive medical skills. But she did not savour people with high tempers or people who created unnecessary drama out of a situation that didn't require excessive emotion.

She'd bet the next two weeks were going to be interesting. 'Would you like to tell me about how you're going with the feeding and caring for Isabella, and then we'll prepare for your flight.'

One hour later, not two, there was a knock at the door and Sofia threw up her hands. 'I don't want to see him. I'm not ready. How typical that he is early. I hate him.'

Cleo stood and then froze in horror as a tall, powerful, darkly handsome man strode in. Sofia's cousin Felipe was also *her* Felipe from Saturday night!

Cold shock widened her eyes as she tried to make sense of nonsense. The man she'd tried to forget after one night of sensual discovery and pure abandonment crossed the room to face her and she felt the blood drain from her face.

Felipe lifted his strong chin and a vein at the side of his strong jaw pulsed. There was no trace of a smile on those sensual lips. He'd known! He'd specifically arranged to hire her from the agency. Without warning her.

Mortification flooded her but the face she kept turned his way by sheer will remained expressionless. Just like his.

'Sister Cleo Wren. I am Felipe Antonio Alcala Gonzales. Sofia's cousin.'

'I see,' was all she could manage.

It really was a shame the embarrassment didn't stop the invisible, floating warmth that settled over her like a red cape, just like a teasing taunt from the toreador, she thought bitterly. *Olé*, you goose, Cleo. Another betrayal with lies. Or enormous omissions at least. What was going on?

But that didn't stop her body thrumming with a tragic awareness of him.

Typically, his thigh-length coat fitted perfectly over immaculately tailored trousers and his long hair was tied tightly back with a plain leather thong, making his high cheekbones stand out in the bright light flooding through the window. She thought of the serious, deeply driven man of the dance and saw him in this man.

There had been no mention of great wealth or the name Gonzales when they'd met.

Nothing of the seductive lover who had charmed and then discarded her. Her legs wanted to run but Sofia would want to know why so she stayed motionless. Calm. Her face a tight mask.

He lifted one long elegant hand assertively towards her to shake hands, and she remembered that every time they'd touched she had been left with a tremor of want.

No way.

Face neutral, Cleo declined to extend her own fingers and doggedly met his dark eyes head on. His narrowed gaze bored into hers as his fingers dropped and moved to clasp together behind his straight back. A stance that suited him. Head of the family after all.

Your move, Don Felipe. I'm certainly not sure what we should do now. Her eyes narrowed at his arrogant appraisal of the situation. Yep, still a conquistador out to conquer new territory. Well, she wasn't about to be conquered. Again. Or lied to. Again.

Her usual resistance to male advances that had melted on Saturday night clanged into place like the gate of a walled city. She almost sagged with relief as she felt clean distance separating any desire she might have had to bury her head in his chest and just inhale the male scent of him. *In fact,* you *are not the man I had fantasies about.*

He'd talked of his dancing. His love for his grandmother. Nothing of his aristocratic background. Nothing of his real life. But at the time she'd accepted that for they had been strangers, and lovers for one night only.

But that was done. Finished, and here he was pretending they'd just met. And was she to do the same? Begin a lie? Like her husband had? She hated lies. Therefore she hated him. Most freeing.

Phew.

Immunity.

All that in seconds that seemed to drag on for a lifetime.

On the bed Sofia shifted and Cleo turned her head. She saw the bitter flash of defiance and the expression on her client's face made their familial resemblance more striking. And worrying.

Sofia turned a look of loathing on the man and threw up her hands. 'Pah. What are you doing here so early?' But there was a trace of tears in the loudly defiant cry. 'I change my mind and stay here.'

Looking at these two, Cleo knew she could kiss goodbye to any quiet life in the next weeks if she didn't drop this assignment. Something it would be crazy not to do now that she knew who Sofia's dastardly cousin was.

She saw the tremor in Sofia's tight fingers and felt the girl's anguish. What had he done to her? What was really going on here? Had she got her impressions of Felipe so badly wrong, everywhere? Had she made the biggest mistake ever in her assessment of the man she'd given herself to?

A tilt of Felipe's aristocratic black head. 'It is not for you to tell me to come, or go, cousin.' Said quietly and confirmed officially for Cleo that Felipe was her VIP employer.

'I don't want you here.' Sofia was crying now and edging towards hysteria and Cleo narrowed her gaze. Whatever he had done it needed to stop now.

Cleo stepped between them. 'Don Felipe.' Her voice cut across the emotion in the room with a quiet crispness. 'My client is upset. Perhaps we could speak outside in the corridor. It is not good for the baby or Sofia to be distraught like this.'

He paused. Narrowed his eyes at her and then after a long, tense pause he nodded. Gestured with his hand. 'After you.' The sardonic tone in the agreement was not lost on her.

Well, she had stepped into the line of fire. Not the first time she'd done that for a patient and it wouldn't be the last.

Unless she died of embarrassment in this hospital today.

Cleo felt his eyes on her back the whole way out the door. She didn't turn until she heard the click of the latch behind him.

Then a vivid flashback of the last time he'd come up behind her and touched her bare shoulder flashed into her brain and she spun quickly to face him.

Not happening again! 'So, you are the wicked older cousin?'

He inclined his head. 'It is my lot in life to protect my family from charlatans and that is what her fiancé was.' He ran his hands through his hair as if exasperated. 'Already the swindler had installed his mistress into Sofia's apartment.'

Good grief. Cleo raised her brows and said curtly, 'Well, I would hope that's come to an end!'

He smiled but there was no amusement in it and Cleo shivered at the implacable look in his eyes. 'Indeed.' He pulled some keys from his pocket and shook them so they rattled. 'Eviction was swift.'

Okay, but… 'Why must Sofia go to Spain now? She is still exhausted from the birth.'

His face remained inscrutable but before he could conceal the emotion, his eyes showed immense sadness. 'Because, if you remember me telling you this, our shared grandmother is dying. It is her wish that before she departs this earth she sees Sofia and has time to know her babe.'

His gaze captured hers and there was no wavering as he said very slowly and clearly, 'I will make this happen for my grandmother, the woman who cared for me like a mother.' She remembered everything he'd told her that night. For a moment she just hadn't been sure what was truth and what was lies once she'd realised who he really was. Except the devastated look in his eyes was clearly genuine.

Then he cast an impatient glance at the door before facing her again. 'Despite what is between us, Sofia trusts you. And she, too, is important, which is why I arranged for you to come. We must work with that and pretend that Saturday night never happened.'

Despite herself, she felt a stab of loss. But, yes, it would be much easier that he concurred with her own thoughts. And it was good he agreed Sofia was important. 'How ill is your grandmother?'

'The cancer has spread through her body. We are giving palliative treatment and she refuses any other care. I believe she has weeks, not months to live. If that long.'

That explained his determination to leave today. 'Thank you for your honesty.' In this instance anyway.

It looked like they were off to Spain. 'I think we can return to Sofia and help her prepare for the departure.'

He didn't answer, just stepped to the door and opened it for her.

Felipe followed her into the room. 'Your midwife will accompany you and be your advocate.' He moved to the window and crossed his arms.

Sofia's dark eyes still glinted with tears but she had composed herself and was sitting straight in the bed. '*Sí*. If I am to do this without my fiancé…' a venomous look Don Felipe's way '… I choose my own assistant. This woman is on my side!'

'Your fiancé.' A disgusted aside spoken quietly, though it carried clearly. 'He was a bad man.'

'Not until you offered him money to leave me.' Another glare from Sofia at her cousin. Then a beseeching glance at Cleo. 'See why I need you to help me leave if I decide I don't want to stay in Spain after all, Cleo?'

Cleo forced herself to keep her eyes on the young woman and not glance at Don Felipe. For she was determined that was how she would think of him now. 'Is there a reason you wouldn't be able to leave if you wished?'

'Ask him.' A jerk of Sofia's defiant head.

Now she allowed her face to turn. Met his gaze squarely. Said very quietly in question, 'Don Felipe?'

'Please. Call me Felipe.' He shrugged, though his eyes glinted with suppressed emotion.

But which Felipe? Cleo thought acidly. She was tempted to ask him that, but professionalism won.

'Is Sofia free to leave Spain if she wishes?'

'Sofia may come and go as she pleases. We do not kidnap people in Spain. Neither do we hold them against their will. Just as soon as she sees her grandmother, she can decide what she wants to do. Though I would prefer she stay until the end.'

The two cousins glared at each other. He continued, 'My cousin has her own resources, after all.'

Cleo suspected Felipe and Sofia's grandmother was really at the heart of their antagonism.

The question remained: Could she still get involved with this man? Again? A man who had left her without him feeling it was important enough to divulge who he really was? A man she had a weakness for? Though even now, for that affront, she could see why, if he was head of an extremely wealthy family, he'd have just been slumming it with her. A lowering thought and one that certainly took off some of the shine. And a good reason to stay at arm's length for the duration of her employment by him. Perhaps the grandmother had sent Felipe. That made sense.

Again, she assessed the young mum, the baby and the man with his arms folded across his chest.

Someone had to support Sofia.

And she knew Felipe could be ruthless in his chosen path. Obviously.

Right, then. 'Don Felipe, when were you hoping to leave?' *This time.* She wasn't calling him Felipe. He could deal with that.

'We leave today. Four p.m. If Sofia can be ready.' So reasonable. Why did she feel that reasonableness was only skin-deep?

She could be reasonable, too. 'I agree to accompany Sofia for the next two weeks. If we are to leave in a few hours perhaps you could give us a little more time alone to discuss matters pertinent to women, babies and midwives?' She glanced at her watch. 'Sofia says you are here an hour early.'

He leaned forward off the wall and raised his dark brows at her.

His face held a gentle warning and possibly, which irritated her beyond all measure, a small amount of amusement. 'I will leave and return in an hour. Or Sofia will text me when you have finished your discussion. On our way to the airport we can transport you to your lodgings to retrieve your suitcase and passport.'

Lucky she'd already packed, Cleo thought with acerbity. It wouldn't take that long to hand over her cat and empty the fridge of perishables, but she wasn't telling him that. 'That won't work. I'll need at least an hour.' His expectation that her needs were not important to him rankled. She wanted to rankle him right back.

It was as if he guessed that. 'Then we will come,' he said silkily, 'when you are able to be prepared.' There was definitely amusement at her expense in his eyes.

Oh, she was prepared—just not instantly biddable.

He crossed the room to the door in three long strides and the door closed softly behind him.

Cleo's hands tightened on the chair back for extra support where she stood.

'I hate that man,' Sofia spat.

I think I do, too, Cleo thought, but she wasn't quite sure.

Sofia hadn't finished. 'His father was a rich pig, powerful and arrogant. Hard. I ran away from him. I had not thought Felipe was just the same, but I can see now he is.'

'Is Felipe really so powerful?'

'Very. The family has a massive fortune and Felipe manages most of it now my grandmother is old. She wants him to marry and has been parading aristocratic Catalonian women in front of him for years.'

Cleo refused to think about that for the moment.

'And she is dying, your cousin said.'

Sofia's beautiful eyes clouded. '*Sí*. But I don't want to believe him.'

Cleo had seen his face when he'd told her. She believed him.

CHAPTER SEVEN

FELIPE WALKED AWAY from his cousin's room and stabbed the elevator button with controlled force.

Cleo Wren.

The woman he had seduced, and been seduced by. He had risen from her bed before dawn yesterday. He had stood outside her flat and looked up at her window like a lovelorn fool. He, who never looked back at his rare, brief liaisons. He was still shocked at himself, picking up an unknown woman and sleeping with her. Or rather not sleeping. It had been as if he could not get enough of her. What was it about Cleo that had made her so irresistible to him? Now was not the time to find out.

His mind had drifted, too, during his busy day on Sunday, and he had looked back at the night before with sweetness and yearned, in the few brief moments he'd had to himself, to see her again. But no time had landed in his lap.

He had known he could not stay in Australia and he did her no favours by extending their connection. Responsibilities had slapped him from the time he'd left her door.

To his disgust, being near her again still nipped at his skin like static electricity and drew his eye with instant recognition of the beat between them.

Memories pounded him again of that night. Those brilliant blue eyes, and the flash of matching colour below her chin. He remembered slowly pulling the blue scarf from that sweet throat.

It felt like only an hour ago and he could still feel the softness of her skin beneath his fingers. The shock of actually seeing her again had been almost as great as that on her own face when she had seen him.

And he'd had prior knowledge that she would be there. Had sanctioned it with the agency.

There could surely be only one midwife called Cleo in the area. He had immediately recognised the name when Sofia had mentioned her, had put the pieces together, and at least had had a few hours' incredulous warning.

She'd refused to shake his hand.

He knew why. He had known they would meet again and not warned her. The unexpected trust he'd been gifted on Saturday night had been shattered and he felt its loss keenly.

Further entanglement would only hurt them both. And be professionally unsound.

For now, sadly, he feared the affront to Cleo

had been greater than he'd intended from an albeit incredible and mutually sharing one-night encounter. Now they both would have to put such thoughts and actions behind them.

Forget.

He almost laughed out loud at that.

Her sweetness could never be forgotten. He'd thought distance would help there but even that was not to be now.

If there was to be any time to explore further what lay between them, it would be after his cousin's safe arrival in Spain, and definitely after Cleo's fortnight in his employ was complete.

It would be best if the time didn't come at all, for he feared to create an imbalanced disaster between two people who lived on opposite sides of the world and came from completely different cultures. Her life was one of freedom of choice, while his was filled with duties and responsibilities. Yet for one night she had allowed him to be the dancer, the lover, the man, and not the doctor of terminally ill patients, the evil cousin, the director of many companies or the head of his ancient family.

With Cleo he could be just Felipe.

His driver, a small, dark, impassive-faced man, opened the door of the car as he strode towards it. 'Take me to the hotel, Carlos. I will remain there until they call. Then proceed to Sofia's flat.' He tossed the keys to his man. 'You will acquire my cousin's luggage, which should be packed by now, and stow it in the boot and then return for me.'

'*Sí*, Don Felipe.'

Felipe climbed into the rear of the vehicle and closed his eyes as he rested his head back against the seat.

Yet it wasn't the enormous list of tasks he needed to complete before they left today that occupied his mind. It was the almost overpowering urge to sweep the midwife up in his arms and hold her against his chest. To thank God he'd found her again.

Fifteen minutes ago everything in his power had been used to stop that action.

She had seemed immune to him, yet he'd sensed she was angry and hurt behind her so-professional face. The watchful eyes and smooth lines of Cleo's cool face had remained outwardly calm and he'd been unable to read anything. But she'd refused to touch his hand.

Yes, she was an independent woman who stood for everything Diego loved about the liberated Australian society. A society's laxness his grandmother was so sure had ruined his cousin Sofia for ever.

When all this was over, and Cleo had returned back to her own country, he doubted he would ever forget the place he had met this woman.

For now, he must not allow himself to think of

Cleo, because his loyalties lay elsewhere with his work, his family and his responsibilities. He had to continue to callously walk away.

No wonder she wouldn't allow his touch.

Yes, it was his family he should be thinking of. Sofia's sudden engagement should have overridden his daily life and his hospice work. It was his responsibility to watch over the decisions of his family and his grandmother's large estate, and he had failed his cousin.

So he had come to make matters right.

And had found Cleo.

Fate was definitely laughing at him. He hoped not at her, too. Because she didn't deserve it.

He grimaced at his grandmother's insistence that he had to be the one to come for Sofia. She knew how much he'd disliked leaving her now the cancer was back. Though there was truth in the fact his cousin would have refused to go with Diego, which was the solution Felipe had initially suggested.

They'd be back in Spain in twenty-four hours and they would be bringing with them an adorable newborn great-granddaughter and a smile to his grandmother's face.

They would also be bringing Cleo Wren and what the ramifications of that would be only time would tell.

CHAPTER EIGHT

REFUSING TO BE distracted by thoughts of a certain man, and with the discussion of the needs of babies and the cares of women who had just given birth, Cleo and Sofia regained their warm understanding of each other. And Cleo practised her Spanish. Though apparently Spanish was different to Catalan.

Baby Isabella had taken to breastfeeding with gusto but the baby's idea of settling after her feed still needed some work.

When Cleo glanced at her watch she saw that their allocated sixty minutes had already passed.

Dark strands of Sofia's hair had fallen across her forehead and she brushed them back petulantly as Cleo reminded her of the time.

'Should you ring him?'

'If I must. But I prefer to text.'

'The sooner we leave here, the sooner you and Isabella can find some routine again in your new home. That's important.'

The young woman nodded and pulled out her phone.

When she'd finished stabbing at the screen she threw the object onto the side table as if it annoyed her.

Cleo studied her thoughtfully. 'Why don't you relax in the shower while we wait for your cousin to arrive? I can watch Isabella and you will feel fresh for the flight.'

Sofia's grimace lightened. 'Yes. I would like that. And to dress in my travel clothes, not pyjamas.'

'Indeed. You are a powerful lioness, after all.' They smiled at each other.

'When you are ready, I will go as I need to close up my flat before he tells me I am not prepared and scoops me up from the footpath,' Cleo said.

Sofia looked up from assembling her bathroom bag. She smiled over her shoulder. 'You think he will scoop you up?'

'Like a big black falcon coming in to land.' Cleo laughed.

Sofia said, 'I like you.'

'And I like you. We will have a very pleasant time settling you back in Spain.'

Sofia raised her hand to her throat and closed her eyes briefly. 'As long as they do not try to marry me off to someone suitable when we get there. Like his father tried to do. I may not wish to stay then.'

'Then you will go elsewhere.' Cleo saw the worry on her face and felt for her. 'I will help you with whatever you need.'

'Yes.' Sofia nodded thoughtfully. 'I am surprisingly reassured by that.' And turned away to enter the bathroom.

Cleo watched her go. 'I'm glad.' She just hoped she could hold up her end of the bargain. When all was said and done she would be under the authority of an influential and prominent family, in a foreign country with a man who had known her intimately.

She just hoped nobody else knew about that.

And she'd be alone to deal with it all.

No. She wasn't really alone. There was phone access to Sir Reginald and Angie if she needed it.

When Sofia reappeared from the bathroom with impeccable make-up, in a comfortable dress of divine cut with front buttons for easy breastfeeding, it coincided with the tall form of Don Felipe framed imposingly in the doorway.

Cleo decided he did it on purpose and chose to show she wasn't impressed. 'Ah. My lift has arrived.'

The 'lift' blinked at her dismissive tone and she smiled sweetly. It seemed the disadvantage at which she found herself whenever she was with him brought out the worst in her.

He tilted his head, an amused glint in his eye. 'My driver will transport you.'

'Have I offended you?' Damn it. She would not be overawed that he was her employer. And that that was all he could be.

'Me? Offended? Why would you think that?' Then he smiled sardonically. 'I've told him where you live.' His mocking drawl made her eyes narrow and she turned back to her client, hoping she hadn't heard the exchange.

But in all honesty she shouldn't have baited him first.

Thankfully, Sofia was busy with Isabella, who had woken and was gazing wide-eyed up at her mother. Sofia could not hear or see anything except her daughter at that moment. Thank goodness.

'I'll see you at the airport, Sofia. Do we need to stop at the shops on my way home? I know we have baby supplies for the flight but is there anything else you wish for?'

Sofia looked thoughtful. 'This is Australia. Vegemite and Tim Tam biscuits?'

'I'll get some at the airport. I saw a huge stand there last week.'

Don Felipe lifted his head. 'We will not go through that part of the airport.'

'Oh.' More sweet smiling. 'Well, then, I'll ask your driver to stop on the way to my flat.'

Sofia shot her cousin a smug look. '*Gràcies*, Cleo.'

'*De nada*, Sofia.' The equivalent of *You're welcome* in Spanish fitted so perfectly there.

They smiled at each other. Felipe looked on impassively at the rapport between the two women and she hoped he felt outgunned.

Cleo waved. 'I'd better go.' She glanced at the man at the door. 'I have a few things to finalise.'

'*Sí.* One hour's worth,' he said dryly.

She nodded coolly as she walked past him.

'While we wait for you, I will ensure Sofia has been discharged by the doctors.'

Cleo had already checked but she said nothing. It would stop him following her.

Exactly an hour after she'd been dropped off at her flat a black car pulled up beside her on the footpath. The large male in the rear seat alighted to tower over her. Her one small cabin bag made Felipe's eyebrows rise.

'You travel lightly.'

'Yes.' She stepped back as if checking to see if the door looked shut behind her but really to increase the space between them. 'A useful skill in my profession.'

The driver had scurried to the rear door and

was holding it open. Felipe returned to the other side of the car.

There were four large seats in the back, Sofia and Isabella in her safety bassinet in the two rear-facing seats.

That left her to sit next to Felipe facing forward. She wondered if she could ask to sit in the front with the driver. She called herself a coward under her breath and slid in.

Once seated and settled she concentrated on Sofia. 'Did you have any issues strapping Isabella into the safety harness?'

The young woman rolled her eyes. 'My cousin took control of that.'

'I have done this before,' Felipe stated impassively as his driver shut Cleo's door.

'Ah. You have children, Don Felipe?'

A narrow gaze. 'No.'

He'd already told her he was unmarried but he had kept plenty of other things from her. Perhaps he had a brood of children by other women he wasn't married to? Probably not. She smiled at her own silliness. Cleo checked the baby. 'She looks nicely settled.'

Not how the mother looked, Cleo thought. Mutinous described that better. Obviously there'd been some dispute between the cousins.

Barely any words passed between the occupants during the trip to the airport but the closeness of Felipe's hip to hers brought a warmth to her belly that she tried unsuccessfully to banish. Sitting next to a stranger she'd had passionate sex with pinged right outside her comfort zone. She didn't know where to look.

His strong, muscular thigh next to hers reminded her how easily he'd carried her to her bedroom.

Those long, elegant fingers reminded her he'd stroked every inch of her.

While bulging biceps that almost touched her own reminded her how he had leaned over her with the weight of his hard, muscular body on those very arms.

Good grief, this was crazy thinking! What on earth was she doing, working for this man?

By the time they arrived at the airport Cleo hoped the flight would be less fraught with tension or they would all have dull pains in the middle of their foreheads when they landed in Barcelona.

They passed swiftly through customs and returned to the car to drive across the tarmac to their aircraft. This was Cleo's first private flight, though she had escorted patients in smaller commercial aircraft.

Once on board, the cabin crew met Felipe and Sofia with warmth and respect, and kindness towards Cleo, who thought again how little they needed her with all this back-up available. But then she thought of Sofia's vulnerability and was glad she'd come.

Felipe had disappeared almost immediately after they came on board and stated he would see them later.

She wasn't sure if he was working or resting but he proved true to his word as they prepared for take-off.

Which made everything much more relaxed at the rear of the aircraft.

As they flew into the night the baby travelled well, soothed by the slight rocking of the aircraft near the tail, and they'd managed perfect privacy for Sofia to feed Isabella and then get some sleep, which helped everyone.

Cleo had even managed four straight hours of sleep herself, in the reclining seat adjacent to her charge. The delightful cabin stewardess had promised to wake Cleo if Isabella stirred, and had proved wonderfully reliable in her promise.

After the next feed Cleo tucked mother and baby in to sleep once more but found herself awake and restless.

Peppermint tea. Her tongue felt glued to the top of her mouth. She'd kill for peppermint tea.

The stewardess had disappeared and Cleo wasn't a bell-pusher so she walked quietly towards the curtains ahead. When she pulled aside the curtain, instead of a galley for meal preparations, as she expected, she found a small circular lounge room and Felipe.

He looked up. Black eyes and black lashes, a flash of remembered heat in his harsh gaze and then it was gone, though his mouth had softened. Apparently whatever business he'd been concentrating on hadn't been fun.

She touched her hair. Smoothed the bump over the band that held it free of her face. Okay, she thought when the strands had been tidied, she looked as professional as possible.

The look he gave her was anything but professional. Though, to be fair, he hadn't expected her.

And she'd just waltzed in. Heat rushed to her cheeks but before she could pull back, he stood.

'Come in. I owe you an apology.'

She wanted to turn her back on him. Hide her hot face at least. Of course, as an employee, she didn't do any of those things. She lifted her chin instead. Smiled slightly, although it felt like it needed to crack through layers of cement before it broke through. 'I'm just looking for peppermint tea. Not an apology.'

'How like the Cleo I met. So straight to the point,' he mused.

That irked her but her voice stayed level. 'How would you know what I'm like? We barely spoke.'

The heat returned to his eyes and his slow smile, though not disrespectful, brought heat flooding back like a blowtorch against her skin.

'Let's not talk again, then.' There, there was that softer, more playful Felipe she remembered.

Unwanted memories flooded her and her fingers clenched by her sides. 'No, we can't do that. Your cousin is my client. She has appraised me of your many influential connections, and I am just the nurse.'

Peripherally she saw those beautiful shoulders rise and fall in a careless shrug but she couldn't take her eyes off his face. He waggled his brows. 'My family is old and distinguished, yes, but you will never be just a nurse.'

He was making fun of her. Being silly. The spell broke. 'I'm going home to Australia in two weeks. The less in-depth we "not talk" the better.' She glanced around. 'I'll just find some tea and go.'

He studied her for a long moment, then reached over and pressed a bell. The stewardess appeared instantly. 'Peppermint tea for Sister Wren, please, Mari.'

She nodded at him and smiled at Cleo. 'At once, Don Felipe.' The woman disappeared.

'Please, take a seat. At least have your tea here.'

Cleo didn't want to drink tea with him watching her. She wanted to take her tea and hide. Blow this.

Her chin lifted. 'I believe I don't deserve to feel at a disadvantage. I'm doing a job and, if I'm allowed the space, I will do it well.'

His face turned serious as he leaned forward. 'My apologies if you feel at a disadvantage. There is no disadvantage to you that I am not feeling as well. Please, stay for a few moments.' He waited for her to consider that.

Reluctantly, she sat, straight backed, on one of the lounges. It wasn't comfortable in that position but at least there was a shelf to put her tea on when it came. And it wasn't within reaching distance of him.

'How are Sofia and the baby?' His voice was quiet. Conversational. As if considerate of her equilibrium. Well, thank goodness for that. Maybe they had got off on the wrong foot today with all the underlying emotions.

She didn't want to be the creator of the unneeded drama she disliked so much. They were both in this together, after all.

She collected her thoughts. Concentrated on providing a sensible answer. 'Settled. They have slept well between feeds.'

'And you?'

She looked up. 'A couple of hours as well. Thank you. Your aircraft is comfortable and your staff very helpful. Do you sleep on flights?'

'I don't sleep much at all.' Another raised brow. Again, her cheeks heated. She could attest to that.

Darn it, she just knew that when she lifted her eyes from her lap he would be watching her with a wicked smile on his face. One that she badly wanted to wipe off. She looked up. Yep.

Instead, to the surprise of both of them, she laughed. 'Boy, this is awkward.'

The tension in his shoulders seemed to fall away. A slow smile, his austere face softening into that of another man. That other man. 'Thank you for your honesty. You are good for me, Cleo. I try not to be so serious with you.'

'Can I ask a question?'

He shrugged, the smile still playing around his lips. 'I do not have to answer you but yes.'

'Why didn't you tell me who you really were and why you were in Australia?'

He was silent and she thought he wasn't going to answer. She hadn't really expected him to. 'Because that was not who I was when I was with you. And it felt good.'

She remembered the look in his eyes when she'd changed her mind about shutting him out to inviting him into her home. The connection of two damaged people that had shimmered between them. And that's enough of that, she told herself, or she'd be feeling sorry for him and she wasn't ready for that.

She changed the subject quickly. 'One more.'

He nodded.

'Was it the right thing to remove Sofia from her fiancé at this crucial time?'

'Yes.' No hesitation. Implacable. He leaned

closer. 'The man…' his lip curled over the word 'man', his voice pitched very low so as not to carry '…apart from the mistress I already mentioned, had already begun to siphon money from her bank account. Large amounts Sofia had not agreed to. His removal was just in time.'

Cleo blew out a long breath. What a sleaze. Poor Sofia. No. Lucky Sofia. She had a family who supported her, even if autocratically. When Cleo's ex-husband had left her broke and brokenhearted for another woman, she'd had no family to save her. But she'd had her friends. Jen, for one.

'Let us talk about ourselves instead of Sofia.' Felipe's voice cut into her thoughts. She stilled at the velvet tone of his words.

Brought her head up. 'I don't think so.'

He leaned forward. 'Do not be embarrassed.'

With a swish of the curtains the stewardess arrived with a loaded tray and Felipe sat back. Even from a few paces away Cleo could smell the peppermint. A selection of tiny sandwiches sat on a plate to the left and round sugar biscuits to the right.

Cleo forced a smile. 'Thank you.'

The stewardess nodded. *'De nada.'* Then turned and disappeared again. Could Cleo pick up the tray and walk away? She could.

But she didn't. 'I'm not embarrassed.' Much. 'As you said at the time, what happened was between consenting adults.' She waved her free hand. 'Now that night is over, and there is no more consent.'

But she didn't quite meet his eyes.

'But it is hard to pretend that I did not taste your sweetness or spend a night in your bed.'

Now she stood. To heck with the tea. 'I'm sure you are perfectly capable of subterfuge, Don Felipe.' She raised her own brows pointedly. 'What's the alternative?' That she be at his sexual beck and call while in Barcelona? Not happening.

'Of course. You're right.' He made a low noise in his throat. 'But I wonder now if this can be hidden? When I watch you move I can think only of what lies beneath your clothes.' She gasped and his hand immediately wiped that comment away. 'I should not have said that. My apologies again.'

She couldn't rid herself of it so easily. 'I regret that you are in this position,' she said stiffly. But it wasn't like she hadn't thought about it herself. Repeatedly.

'And yet I do not regret anything.' He stood. 'Except not being more honest with you. I will leave you to have your tea in peace.'

The steam from the ornate spout of the teapot rose between them like a wall. 'Thank you.' Cleo looked away from him to the waiting cup, then back.

Felipe turned as quietly as she knew he could.

And the way he walked carried her straight back to a steamy flamenco dance floor and a serious case of the wants.

Had she done the right thing in shutting him down?

Shutting down any discussion about something that could only bring discomfort to both of them. She didn't think so. There had been a spark, well, a roaring flame, actually, between them, which left an ache somewhere in her chest, but he was of the aristocracy and lived in Spain.

She had her own life, seventeen thousand kilometres away from him. And to cap it all off, she was temporarily working for the man.

But most of all, she suspected, with how quickly she had fallen under his spell, she could be hurt far worse than her ex-husband had hurt her if she let herself get in any deeper.

CHAPTER NINE

FELIPE WALKED AWAY from Cleo because if he didn't, he could quite conceivably reach out and pull her into his arms and forget all restraint. Apart from being morally despicable, it would be the absolute worst thing he could do in view of the coming two weeks of forced proximity.

Yet a part of him said this was his aircraft, his staff, and as long as she agreed to him kissing her then most of those with them were asleep and would not know.

He could have pressed the button for privacy so nobody would have entered the lounge, and once he had her in his arms she would have been his.

Which was exactly the sort of thing his father would have done. He had used women and discarded them, including those who'd worked for him. Both for pleasure and for political gain. This lack of principles was not Felipe's way and had strengthened the rift between father and son when Felipe had made his disgust known. It was not how he wanted to live his life.

But morality was a good enough reason not to take Cleo into his arms again.

He paused at one of the exit doors and leaned his hand against the bulkhead. Stared blindly out through the oval window into the blackness beyond and searched for answers.

Even now, he could feel the soft weight of her in his arms, the warmth beneath his fingers as he traced the line of her shoulder, the curve of her cheek, the feel of a pulse beating in secret places and the absolute silk of her thighs.

He shook himself. This was not normal. He'd never felt such honesty between himself and a woman as he had on Saturday night—and now that was shattered because she felt he had tricked her by withholding his real identity.

Certainly, Cleo had not been chasing the Gonzales name or fortune, unlike many others in his past. And even now, when she knew who he was, he could tell that wealth was the least of his attraction to her. But there was still that sizzling chemistry between them, that moment when she'd looked at him and spoken with absolute truth, 'Boy, this is awkward.' He smiled at the memory. His Cleo. She remembered his body as well.

Something of this woman had attached itself to him and created a bond that he'd walked away from, and now fate had sprung him back to her side like an elastic band. Snapping them together in the closeness of Sofia's orbit.

The question was, did he fight to stay or fight to get away?

Carlos appeared beside him. 'Don Felipe? May I do anything for you?'

'No. Rest, Carlos. I will go to my suite.' For a cold shower, though he didn't say it. 'Thank you.'

CHAPTER TEN

BARCELONA GREETED THE travellers with blue skies, a gentle tepid breeze and a blaze of colour as they stepped onto the tarmac from the aircraft.

Travelling via private jet had been a whole new experience for Cleo and certainly less bothersome than following a wheelchair through customs.

Except for the fact that the man she'd slept with owned the plane and twenty-four hours flight time was a long time in Felipe's aircraft.

She still wasn't sure how she was going to stay sane for the next two weeks.

She appreciated the fact that Felipe had left her to drink her tea in peace.

Unfortunately, peace had been hard to come by and she'd spent many hours nervous she would run into him again.

You couldn't just forget about a man you'd recently shared the most intimate moments with.

The most improbable thing about this whole situation was that she'd actually had her first one-night stand, for goodness' sake. She'd have to blame it on the flamenco. The wicked dance was probably designed for just that reason. Blatant sensual arousal.

Now, watching the muscled back and strong shoulders of the man in front as he carried the baby's bassinet, there were tantalising glimpses of that stalking arrogant walk that had so mesmerised her that night.

But she was here for two weeks to help Sofia. She needed to stay concentrated on that goal. She could do that. She was a professional. Her gaze shifted to Sofia, who followed her baby's bassinet mutinously. Cleo dropped back to allow the warring parties to go ahead.

Sofia had shared her disquiet already, at returning to Spain, and Cleo had felt like saying, *Why don't the two of us just go home to Australia, then?* Man, she'd been so tempted.

But that wasn't her job.

Her job was to ignore any awkward past between the boss and herself and get Sofia settled so she could see her grandmother. Then her client could decide what she wanted to do.

Five minutes later they were gliding through heavy traffic as they were swept from the airport to the city in another of Felipe's cars. Same driver.

Unlike Felipe's black limousines, everywhere else in Barcelona lay with a palette of colour.

Flower beds, apartments, avant-garde artworks standing in parks or at street corners, bright hues shone and lifted the ordinary to the extraordinary. Even advertising billboards seemed bigger and more vibrant.

Cleo had seen photos of the city online, but in the frolicsome flesh Barcelona pulsed with sunshine and fun. She wished she'd come with Jen and not with Felipe and Sofia.

Before she'd realised who paid her wages, she'd hoped to explore Gaudi's gardens and architecture towards the end of her stay. She did wonder if keeping her head above the emotional water of avoiding Felipe would impact on any light-hearted sightseeing. She'd just have to push through that because she could see now there was so much more of this amazing city to soak in.

Across from her, Sofia fidgeted with a slim diamond ring on her finger and Cleo's heart went out to her. Sofia had told her she didn't believe everything Felipe had said about her ex-fiancé or that he'd taken her money. So he'd arranged for her to see her bankers soon after their arrival here. Despite everything that had happened between herself and Felipe, Cleo did believe him.

Sofia would undoubtedly feel the eyes of the gossips on her. For Sofia, a member of an elite family in the city, she'd be known to many. It would not be comfortable to return home after being heartbroken and made a fool.

Cleo silently agreed it wasn't at all comfortable from the midwife's point of view either.

Though she was far from heartbroken. And she didn't believe Felipe was a bad man. There were no hearts involved in their situation. No, siree. Just a night between two consenting adults. She couldn't even blame alcohol as one glass hadn't caused her to fall into Felipe's arms.

But no one knew, she reassured herself.

As long as Sofia had no idea how hard Cleo worked not to feel embarrassed by Felipe's hip next to hers every time they drove somewhere, then all would be well. She had to believe that.

The tingle of Felipe's gaze infiltrated her awareness, but she refused to turn her head away from the window to acknowledge him. It was hard enough shutting him out. So she stared at the city and gave Sofia privacy with her thoughts as well.

Thankfully, the scenery flew past in myriad colours and surprises and Isabella lay asleep in her bassinet to allow everyone their own thoughts.

Felipe touched her arm. It seemed he would not be ignored.

She turned her head. He sat forward and indicated the streetscape with his long, elegant fingers. 'The most beautiful city in the world.' His smile and his words carried her back to their first walk together.

Ah. A warm memory. She was sorry now that she'd ignored him. It wasn't like her to be petty. 'Just like Sydney.' Their gazes locked. Both smiled and she looked away. That way lay dragons.

Sofia, who'd leaned towards her own window, also wore a slight smile on her parted lips. Perhaps not all her memories of Barcelona were uncomfortable.

The further they drove into the city the brighter Sofia became. Cleo could see Felipe noted his cousin's unconscious uplift of mood but thankfully didn't mention it.

Small mercies, Cleo thought. If these two could forget their differences, life would be easier for all of them.

'We will come back this way later when Sofia has rested. My grandmother lives in the city. My place of residence is a little farther up the mountain at Sarrià-Sant Gervasi.'

'And where am I to be staying?' Sofia asked with a tinge of bitterness that flattened Cleo's hopes of peace.

'You will stay with me in your own apartments for now, until your plans are decided, as will your nurse.'

'Midwife,' Cleo corrected mildly. 'Sofia doesn't need a nurse.' Then before he could answer she said, 'Do we pass your grandmother's home on the way?'

She wondered if Sofia had a Spanish home of her own or other relatives as well as Felipe, even distant ones. Others who could agree with him and help Sofia see she'd needed to come back at least to see her grandmother. She knew Sofia's parents had passed away, but why had Felipe been chosen to go and get her?

'No. Doña Luisa has an apartment in the Eixample Dreta. We do not pass it. Tonight, possibly, we will visit my grandmother once I have ascertained that she is well enough for guests.'

Sofia scowled and turned her head away but didn't say anything. Isabella gave a mewl of distress and Sofia and Cleo both looked across at the bassinet.

The young woman gave an audible exhalation and relaxed her shoulders. 'Like a contraction,' she murmured.

Good girl, Cleo thought, but the comment left her struggling not to laugh out loud.

Felipe's brows furrowed at the joke he was clearly not included in but nobody enlightened him.

'You said you have visited Spain before?' Felipe's voice broke into her thoughts.

'Yes, but not this part of Spain. I've escorted patients from Madrid and Valencia but both were rapid extractions of ill clients and all my concentration was on them.'

'Perhaps after Sofia has found her feet you will have an opportunity to explore.'

'Perhaps. It's up to Sofia.' And how badly I'll need to get back home and away from you for my own peace of mind. Maybe she wouldn't see much of him even if they lived in his house. 'Do you have a place of work?'

'*Sí*. The hospice. Perhaps I will show you.'

She waited but nothing else came. 'Do you have a normal day-to-day job there? What do you do?'

'Ah, I should have said earlier in the aircraft. I am a doctor. Do you have much knowledge of oncology?'

What? The dancer in her mind moved even further away. The unexpected offering of information made her blink. 'A little.'

She thought about two more recent clients she'd met and become friends with. 'Occasionally terminal clients require support to return home after a more rapid decline in health than expected. I believe nothing is more important than to make their comfort and fulfilment of their wishes a priority at the end of life.'

'Yes. Thank you.' Then, almost to himself, 'I should not be surprised you say that.'

'You are an oncologist? And...a hospice director?'

'*Sí*. Both.'

Not a dance artist in your spare time? Oh, she

wished she could say that out loud. But Sofia would hear and ask questions. But he saw the mischief in her eyes and raised his brows in silent query. She shook her head. An oncologist? She wouldn't have guessed it. Yet another contradiction.

'Oncologists and oncology nurses are special people,' she murmured. Well, she'd already guessed he was special.

'*Sí*. As are those who deal with the beginning of life.' Was that a compliment to midwives? Or was that to atone for the 'nurse' comment he'd made earlier?

'We have just completed building a new hospice. Named after my grandmother.'

It all came back to her then from their night together. He'd mentioned the hospice but not that he ran it and had been involved in its creation. She looked at him, seeing his commitment to his job, and another tiny piece of the wall that she'd erected between them fell away.

He didn't notice her change. 'It has taken up a large portion of the last few years. Then when my father died there were even fewer hours in the day as family business intruded.'

Any softening that had lightened the harshness that seemed to be his default expression was gone, though for her peace of mind it was better when he wore an expression of aristocratic hauteur.

It had been recent, his father's death? His role as family head was new, too, then. 'I'm sorry to hear your father also has passed away.' She remembered he had said his mother was gone. So they were both technically orphans, though he was clearly suffering no monetary hardship. Sofia had said he was rich. And he owned his own international aircraft. So why did he make her feel that he needed her?

His face shifted and she felt a wave of sadness emanate from him. 'My grandmother is not a feeble woman and has hung on as long as she could, hence the necessity to speed up Sofia's return.'

'So you said. I'm sorry she is so unwell.'

He inclined his head but didn't look at her. She would have liked to see his face but he'd turned to stare out the window. 'She does not leave her bed much now. I think she will enjoy meeting you. Her contentment at this stage is very important to me.'

'I look forward to meeting her.'

Now he turned his head and studied her. 'Good!'

Was that a warning to not upset his grandmother?

'To your right is the ocean.' And there it was. The end of that subject and the distraction of viewing the port of Barcelona.

Talk about having topic changes on speed dial.

Dutifully she studied the famous Barcelona

seafront. But she accepted it as a good enough place to find some mental space from the man beside her.

Tall white cruise ships and the port. Mountains in the distance, front and back. A blue diamond sea.

They drove through the city, past more brightly painted artworks on street corners, a multifaceted face, an outstretched and oversized hand, and away in the distance on the mountain in front of them she could see a white church high up overlooking the city.

They wound their way through close streets and began to climb in a sweeping motion through avenues to the summit of the mountain. The higher they climbed, the more ornate the iron and stone entries to semi-hidden houses grew.

When they reached one of the most imposing gateways the tall wrought-iron gates swung ponderously open to fold back against the overarching greenery of tree branches.

A short tree-lined gravel road swept them into a circular driveway and the stone villa soared above them in curves, balustrades and high windows that seemed to reach to the sky.

The base of the mansion sat amidst roses, hundreds of flowering roses. It took her breath away.

The house itself ascended three storeys yet seemed higher and spread out backwards. The sparkling bow windows each side of the front door were open and fluttering curtains seemed to wave and flicker a welcome home to its master.

The dozen or so steps that began wide at the driveway where they'd stopped and narrowed as they rose to the huge double door at the top created a grand ascending entrance.

A problem if you were injured or ill, Cleo thought, but noted another, smaller ornate door away to the right at ground level. Maybe that led to a less strenuous entry or perhaps even a lift.

Balconies along each floor above them promised wonderful places to sit with a view over the city below.

She turned to Felipe beside her on the rear seat. 'You have a beautiful house.'

'*Sí*. My grandfather built this for his wife.' His face softened as he looked past her to his home. 'But my grandmother prefers living in the city now that he has gone.' His face stilled as the car halted. 'She lived here until I was old enough to establish my own household then moved to the city.'

Cleo thought it would be lonely living here by yourself. 'Great view,' she murmured as the driver alighted and opened her door.

Some space from Felipe's big body was welcome. She eased out so Sofia could also climb out and by the time the women were standing beside the car Felipe had removed the infant carry part of the bassinet and had lifted Isabella from the car.

A small dark-haired woman glided down the steps, her thin face serious. Another larger blonde woman, who certainly didn't glide but had ramrod-stiff shoulders and the apparent strength to carry them all up the stairs if she wanted to, followed. They were shadowed by two burly younger men in matching waistcoats whom Cleo presumed would bring the luggage.

'*Hola*, Rosa,' their host greeted the thin dark-haired woman.

She dipped a curtsey. '*Buenos días*, Don Felipe.'

'Sister Wren, this is my housekeeper,' he said to Cleo. 'Leave your bags. Rosa will arrange everything.'

Cleo followed Sofia up the steps, Felipe carrying the bassinet, but she was uncomfortably aware that she'd never stayed in such a palatial home before. She was learning so much about the man she'd shared her bed with. Too many more reasons why he had planned to leave her behind.

Once through the large doors he stopped and placed the bassinet gently on a carved wooden chair against one of the walls.

Cleo barely took in the stretch of Italian marble floor and the soaring painted ceiling as she followed Sofia to her daughter.

Sofia began to undo the straps and Cleo slid

the young woman's handbag from her shoulder and held it. The infant grizzled and whimpered until she was lifted into her mother's arms and settled.

Finally, Cleo could observe the tension drain from Sofia's shoulders as she held her baby.

She turned her head sideways to note if Felipe had observed the same. Their eyes met.

It seemed he had. But all he said was, 'Rosa will take you to your rooms and Maria will attend to any laundry needs or other requirements. I have not engaged *mainadera*.' He paused and glanced at Cleo, explaining, 'A nanny…' then back to Sofia '…as you have your own midwife.'

Yes, she'd understood the word for nanny. She had some Spanish, even less Catalan. And French, Italian and German because she needed it in her job. And languages were easy for her to learn.

Sofia drew herself up and faced her cousin. 'You are correct. My child does not need a nanny, she has a mother, but Cleo is my guest.' The words were directed at Felipe.

Cleo smiled at the young mum. 'I can be both. And here's Rosa to show us to your apartment.' Thank goodness.

Felipe ignored Sofia and directed a dark glance at Cleo. 'I will send a message later this afternoon in regard to this evening and my grandmother's ability to receive visitors.'

'Of course,' Cleo agreed, with a careful glance at Sofia and the baby. She'd be glad to get out from between the two warring parties.

CHAPTER ELEVEN

FELIPE WATCHED THEM GO. In fact, he couldn't help watching Cleo's shapely legs and straight back as she easily climbed the stairs. Again. He'd watched her do that before, at her home. He suppressed the sigh he wanted to expel at the stubbornness of his cousin and the stupidity of his libido.

It was his awareness of the midwife that caused him the most distraction. Which was not part of the plan.

Once he was busy with his life, the board meetings, patient consultations, the family businesses, everything that had been interrupted by his grandmother's request to find and bring Sofia home, it would settle down once more, and he needed to resume all that now.

Perhaps he should have arranged for Sofia's parents' house to be prepared and staff installed there rather than bring her here. He told himself that in her present frame of mind whomever he engaged she would have suspected they could not be trusted. Hopefully her rancour towards him would lessen soon, as he was growing weary of it. He was still not sure she'd stay, even if he had made her house available to her, though she'd at least have had her independence, and her midwife to settle her in.

Which meant he wouldn't have had the distraction of Cleo staying in his own house. She still tempted him every time their glances met. Each time he noted the tiniest shift of her body beside him in the car.

A phone buzzed in his pocket and he slid his hand down and lifted it to his ear.

His mouth softened. '*Sí*, Àvia.' He listened as his grandmother launched into excited questions and leaned back against the wall with a slight smile on his face. It had been the right thing to bestir himself and fly to Australia. He hadn't heard her this animated for many weeks. When she finally ran down he gently suggested their plans for the evening if she was up to it. Again, he heard the excitement in her voice and even a proposed menu was shared.

He smiled. 'Shall I bring the Australian midwife, too? Sofia would prefer it if I did, I think.'

He listened as his grandmother agreed. 'As long as you are well enough for her as well, then. Good, and we will see you with your new great-granddaughter at seven for tapas.'

CHAPTER TWELVE

CLEO FOLLOWED SOFIA up the stairs.

Below them she could hear Felipe answer his phone.

With her hand on the ornate wooden rail Cleo had a chance to look around the enormous space that comprised the front door, the entry, with places to sit and wait before you were invited into the inner sanctum of the house, and the soaring dome of the ceiling.

The magnificent angels painted above her head on the ceiling she couldn't study on the move but would take some time later to appreciate the works of art.

When they reached the landing, Rosa turned left and down a hallway, and at the end of the corridor she pushed open a green panelled door.

The room inside opened to a lounge area with a bow window looking over Barcelona away in the distance below. On the opposite side of the room windows showed trees and gardens and blue sky.

The room, in mint green and white, provided a

restful air and obviously feminine overtones and spread larger than Cleo had expected for guest apartments.

'There are three bedrooms here,' Rosa said, in accented English. She nodded at Cleo. 'Yours is to the left, the child next and Doña Sofia has the front room.'

There was a knock at the door and a footman entered at Rosa's call. 'Would you like me to send Maria to unpack for you?' she asked Sofia.

Sofia shook her head, though she drooped as she stood there. 'No. Thank you, Rosa, we will be fine.'

'Then I will order light refreshments to be brought up.'

She turned to Cleo. 'And you. Do you require anything?'

'No. I'm fine, thank you, Rosa,' she said. 'Thank you for your assistance. Your English is wonderful.'

'Don Felipe's mother spoke English.' She left abruptly and the door closed behind her.

Sofia sank down into a chair, clutching her baby, and one lone tear slid down her cheek. 'I don't want to be here. I'm in his house. With his servants. And the father of my child is across the other side of the world.' She looked at Cleo. 'I fell in love with him. He spoiled me, encouraged me to do what I wished, unlike anyone in my family had, and I liked having my own apartment and being able to go where I wished when I wished. Now I am back in Spain. A prisoner in Felipe's house.'

'You are not a prisoner. You are here to see your grandmother.' Cleo crossed to her and perched on the edge of the nearest chair to lean towards her. 'Which is why you insisted I come. To support you. You're tired. It's been a huge twenty-four hours.'

'No kidding,' Sofia grumbled.

'You've kept Isabella happy during a very long flight. Perhaps top up her feed, which will help you feel more relaxed, and then both of you could rest. Build up your strength for tonight.'

Sofia nodded. Sat down with her baby and undid her shirt.

Cleo turned to the luggage. 'I'll unpack the bags while you feed. Then maybe I could settle Isabella to sleep while you lie down and rest.'

Sofia nodded. 'I may feel better if all goes as you say.'

By evening Sofia seemed quite settled in the apartment and her smile had returned. Isabella played model baby with her mother's full attention.

Cleo had discovered Sofia had a house just outside Barcelona, inherited from her parents, but that it was currently closed and without staff.

So perhaps Don Felipe had done the correct

thing to bring her here. A house out of town, without friends or family, might have proved daunting for a new mum with only her baby as company, she thought, but hoped it wouldn't be in her remit to arrange any moves.

Cleo showered and donned her simple cream shift, the one that washed like a dream and never looked as if it had come out of a suitcase. The high-necked style could be a formal floating knee-length frock or almost a uniform if she gathered it in with a belt.

She wore her favourite blue lapis bead necklace and she pulled it out to sit at the neck of the dress to give herself extra confidence. She shouldn't feel she needed it, but who knew how grand Felipe's grandmother was. Especially now she knew how grand Felipe was. This was his world and she wanted to keep her head held high.

'Your necklace is pretty,' Sofia commented as she walked past to take a cup of fresh tea that had arrived.

'It was my mother's. Blue at my neck always helps my thoughts turn into words that flow more easily. I wear it most days.'

'Perhaps I should get myself one so I can tell my cousin what I think of him.'

Cleo laughed. 'I think you do very well without any help. Tell me about your grandmother. How old is she?'

'Doña Luisa is in her early eighties. Though

you wouldn't think it to look at her. She has a beautiful home in the centre of the city. It will be good to show her Isabella. As long as she doesn't harp at me about finding a Catalan husband. And if she is unwell, perhaps I could stay and help her until she is well again.'

She wasn't going to get well again. For some reason Sofia was refusing to believe that. Cleo wasn't going there. Tonight they would see. And as for a husband for Sofia, she had no idea how upper echelon Spanish families arranged marriages and didn't particularly want to know.

'If she is very ill, mortality can make people adjust their needs. Don Felipe mentioned your grandmother is failing fast now. Perhaps the idea of the next generation with a full life ahead of them is a comfort for her at this time.'

Sofia looked suddenly frightened and very young. 'We will see.'

CHAPTER THIRTEEN

A MESSAGE CONVEYED by Rosa arrived after their rest. Felipe had left the house to attend the hospice, but requested everyone to be prepared to leave at seven to visit Doña Luisa.

At five to seven Isabella, in the way of breast-fed babies, created last-minute irreparable damage to the delightful frock she'd been dressed in. Sofia looked as though she would cry. 'She looked so beautiful. We'll be late now.'

Cleo wrapped a bunny rug around the disaster until they could start on the repair. 'She'll need a bath. These things happen. I can help.'

'No. You go down. I will bath her and choose another dress. But you tell my cousin he will have to wait.'

Cleo wondered who'd got the worst job. 'Of course he will wait.'

All afternoon it had sunk in that she was in the principal residence of a Spanish aristocrat she'd slept with. And still fancied. With the suspicion he still fancied her as well. How had she got herself into this?

Cleo blocked the nervous flutter at being the one descending to find the master of the house and checked her handbag. She had everything. More than everything, really. She was a bit of a girl scout and always prepared.

Of course, a minute later when she did pause at the top of the stairs, before searching to find him, Felipe was waiting at the bottom to watch her descend.

Her skin heated enough to know he observed her with extreme concentration. She didn't plan to give him the excitement of tripping and making a fool of herself so she went carefully. No, sedately.

When her shoes touched the marble floor at the bottom of the stairs she lifted her head and, as expected, his gaze sat firmly on her face.

'*Bona nit*, Cleo.'

'Good evening, Don Felipe. Isabella has made her mother late. I've been sent to offer apologies while Sofia changes Isabella's clothes.'

Instead of the impatience she'd half expected, though maybe she was channelling Sofia there and not her own experience, a smile softened his firm features.

'Babies run to their own timetables.'

She tilted her head. 'And how do you know that?'

He shrugged his shoulders and looked at her quizzically. 'I have friends with children.'

'You are the doting uncle type?' It was a question that came out as a statement of disbelief bordering on amusement.

'You don't believe me?'

A shrug. 'Not my place as your employee.' Primly.

'And here I was thinking you were Sofia's guest.'

Now, that was funny. She laughed. His face softened and he smiled back at her.

'Would you like a drink while we wait?' he asked.

Of all the people who needed to stay sober and keep their wits about them it was probably her. 'I don't think so. Thank you.'

'This is Spain. Wine is an institution.'

'Not at this time for me.' Or she'd end up in an institution.

He studied her for a moment longer and then withdrew his phone from his pocket. 'I will let Doña Luisa know we will be a few minutes late.'

He stepped back and Cleo took the opportunity to reassemble her battered shield under the guise of examining the entry. She knew Felipe could be charming when he wished but she had to guard against that. It made him nearly irresistible.

She concentrated on the blue swirls in the marble floor that had been picked up in the columns that ringed the circular room. Towering columns every six feet, floor to ceiling, and she assumed they carried the weight of the dome above. That was some weight.

She moved to one of the spindly-legged velvet three-seaters and sat on one end so she could lean her head against the wall and admire the ceiling. Calm settled over her as she drank in the scene. Truly amazing artwork. This was good. A quiet minute to collect herself and some time to breathe.

In the distance she could hear Felipe murmuring in Catalan but most of her attention stayed on the ceiling above. Rich, vibrant colours depicted gliding angels with red capes. Glorious pale-skinned cherubs with golden curls reached out to a triumphant warrior on his horse holding up a shield and sword. She wondered how he didn't fall off the horse while holding both.

Felipe came and sat down beside her to lean his head back against the wall beside hers, his eyes on the ceiling, too. She felt he was smiling but no way was she going to turn her head to find out. He was too close.

The masculine scent she now associated with him drifted over her, bringing back far too many memories. Still resting her head back against the wall, she asked, 'One of your ancestors?'

'Yes. We're a bloodthirsty lot, my countrymen.' She turned her face to him and noted the glint in his eye when he said, 'And we like to win the wars we engage in.'

'Take the spoils and run?' Their eyes met. Her cheeks warmed. She wouldn't mind taking those words back.

His eyes widened but he resisted teasing her, a small mercy, and she changed the subject. 'Did your grandmother understand why we will be late?'

'Of course. *A baby is a baby.*' He smiled. 'Her words.'

'You are all very patient. Why is Sofia so angry with you? Why doesn't she believe anything you say?'

'Smoother tongues than mine have filled her head with lies. She will eventually learn the truth.' He closed his eyes briefly as if weary. 'I am not patient with that subject. Enough about my silly cousin.' He turned his head and their eyes caught and held. 'There is another subject I am not tired of.'

He smiled and she felt her own lips curve despite the warning bells that began to ring, at first quietly and then more stridently, in her head. A pulse beat in his strong jaw and she had the ridiculous impulse to lift her hand and feel its beat. He was so beautiful a man.

His irresistible mouth came closer.

At that moment they heard a door open upstairs and then footsteps along the corridor above.

Sofia, with Isabella in her arms, appeared at the top of the stairs.

Felipe stood abruptly and Cleo sagged back in what she told herself was relief. She needed to snap out of it.

'Take care, there's plenty of time.' Felipe's voice carried easily up the stairs and ironically Cleo wondered if he was talking to Sofia or to them. She saw the young mum pause as if collecting herself.

Yes, the last thing they needed was Sofia to rush down the steps and fall. Or for Cleo to accept a kiss in Felipe's house while working for the man.

By the time they were all in the car Isabella had gone to sleep and Sofia had her own head resting on the cushions with her eyes shut.

Cleo had her own thoughts to occupy her and was glad Sofia didn't need her input on anything. It was important that her client feel relaxed when they arrived.

Even Felipe seemed to have appreciated that fact.

Twenty minutes later the car stopped in a typical Barcelona street with motorbikes parked in the centre of the road and more mopeds under the trees along the edges of the footpath.

The occasional delivery van zoomed past the tall cream buildings, all seeming to be six to eight storeys high with ornate balconies and roof scrolling. This was obviously one of the quieter and more exclusive inner-city streets. Though on the corner a gorgeous café with tables on the sidewalk had people spilling out onto the street—a family with young children were eating gelato and the parents were laughing as they wiped dribbles of coloured ice from their youngest's face.

For a second Cleo felt the catch in her heart at all the things she'd lost thanks to her own shattered marriage, but she pushed it away. Not here. Not now.

The entrance to Doña Luisa's house lay behind a tall spiked gate that swung inwards when Felipe pushed it.

Beyond lay white marble steps with a red carpet disappearing into the distance. At the sides, speckled grey marble columns matched the grey of the marble walls but frames of cream plasterwork covered the higher reaches and kept everything light as another steeper set of stairs twirled away in a circular climb.

To the right sat an ornate elevator, round roofed, all gleaming wood and brass and glass like something out of an ancient hotel. The doors clanked as Felipe closed the three adults and one baby snugly inside.

With a jolt they shifted upwards, and their cage creaked as it rode to the third floor. The faint aroma of furniture polish and age wasn't unpleasant.

When Felipe opened the ancient elevator doors, they stepped out into an entry hung with red velvet curtains and intricate grey wallpaper, lit by lamps in sconces. A double door opened to the entrance of a large salon.

A massive fireplace, cold and filled with precious brass art objects rather than wood, held a mantel hung with a huge gilt mirror. On the wall priceless paintings broke up the wallpaper and everywhere spindly chairs were empty as if expecting hordes of visitors.

Instead a maid waited. She curtsied to Felipe and Sofia. 'Your grandmother is in the salon.'

Felipe gestured with his hand for them to follow him. 'We'll find our own way, Alba.' The woman inclined her head again and disappeared through a door.

Cleo followed the two cousins and couldn't help the widening of her eyes as her silenced feet trod the glorious Aubusson carpet runner over the paved marble and past glowing ornate furniture. Shimmering oil paintings were lit softly by windows to the outside. It was like a private museum.

The corridor ended in a wood-panelled room with a white sectioned ceiling that curved and drew her eye to the magnificent chandelier in the centre of the roof.

At first she saw the gilded screens, the marble-topped tables and velvet-upholstered chairs sitting on polished parquetry intricately inlaid with different shades of gold and red-brown timber and reflecting the light.

Don Felipe crossed to the chair in front of another unlit fire and leaned down to kiss the wrinkled cheek of the woman who now turned their way.

That was when Cleo saw the small white-haired woman sitting with a dark shawl around her shoulders. She seemed ethereal in her frailty.

'Àvia, Grandmother, I have brought Sofia and Isabella.'

'*Sí.* And you would have been in trouble if you hadn't.' There was a hint of amusement in the dry voice. The woman's gaze went to the dark-haired baby in Sofia's arms. 'She has her mother's hair.'

'And her father's eyes,' Sofia muttered.

Doña Luisa's gaze moved from the child to the mother. 'I hope not. For his were full of avarice.'

'Ávia,' Felipe murmured placatingly, 'Sofia is upset.'

'And I am old and have no patience. Or time.' The white head swivelled. 'And who is this pretty other lady?'

Cleo felt her face flush. Nobody had called her pretty in years.

'The midwife I mentioned,' Felipe said. 'Cleo Wren.' And, yes, there was amusement under his introduction as if he found her blush a reason to smile.

'Miss Wren.'

'It's a pleasure to meet you, Doña Luisa.' Now that she was closer Cleo could see the underlying yellowish tint to the skin. The sunken eyes. Yes, this woman was terminally unwell.

'My grandson tells me you have much experience in caring for the ill and stranded…?' The question hung at the end.

'Indeed. I find it satisfying to help people return home safely when they are vulnerable. At those times people need their family.'

'And you have brought Sofia back home. I am grateful.'

'Your grandson has done all the arranging.'

'Yes. I can see.' Her eyes twinkled as she glanced between Cleo and Felipe. 'I heard this.'

Felipe's head snapped up at that. But Doña Luisa just smiled blandly at him and cast one last look at Cleo. 'You are a sensible woman.'

She turned to Sofia. 'But you, my grandchild…' Her voice trailed off and Cleo had the impression that Doña Luisa did not think Sofia was a sensible woman. 'Forgive me, child. You have suffered a betrayal. I have forgotten what it was to feel strong emotions for a man.'

She looked across and raised her brows at Felipe. 'Except for you, dear grandson. Though sometimes my emotion is frustration. You spend too much time giving to others when I would like to see you care more for your own happiness.'

Her thin arm stretched towards the waiting chairs. 'Sit, Sofia, here next to me, and tell me of your little daughter. She is truly beautiful.'

And Cleo could finally release the tension she'd held over this meeting.

This was why they'd come all this way. For this ill and elderly woman to meet Isabella. As Sofia sat down with the baby in her arms Cleo stepped back.

Felipe had moved behind her to pour a glass of wine and she almost bumped into him. She edged sideways and increased the distance between them.

'Are you sure you wouldn't like to taste my grandmother's Cava?' he murmured.

'Cava?' Words from the past played in her head. *Like Lonia Cava from Catalonia. Wine that tastes of white peach, melon and apple…* His first words to her. After he'd pretended to be a dancer. Didn't he remember?

'Someone offered me that once before.' She pretended she, too, didn't remember it was him.

He frowned at her, as if he sensed her disappointment in him. 'Cava is one of the Catalonian Designation of Origin products. Nowhere else in the world can produce it and call it Cava. My grandmother buys from a local restaurant who make their own.'

She needed something to do with her hands. 'A small one, then. Thank you.' She could at least pretend to unwind.

He reached for another glass and poured an inch of the wine into the glass. At least he was listening.

'Come, we will sit near the window and watch the world go by while they talk.'

He gestured to two large winged chairs with an ornate side table between them.

The red velvet curtains shed a pink glow into her lap as she sat and looked out onto the street above the leafy tops of trees.

The view filled the room with soft light. Peaceful.

The man opposite was not.

'Have you settled into my home?' That sounded very determined.

Cleo looked at him in pretended surprise. 'Yes, thank you.' Why wouldn't she feel settled in the house of a man she'd slept with when she'd thought he was a dancer and who had actually turned out to be a Spanish nobleman pursued by hordes of panting women? 'I'm fine.' She lifted the glass to her lips. 'You?'

His mouth kicked up. She really wished he wouldn't do that.

'I am home.'

'Your grandmother dotes on you.'

An elegant shrug, dismissing any emotion she

might have glimpsed. 'My *àvia* and I have spent a lot of time together.'

His raised brows suggested he'd given her something, so now she could also share. 'And you? Was your childhood happy?'

They'd discussed some things that night in Australia, but hadn't gone into detail. They had been barely acquainted, after all. Why did he want to stretch those boundaries now? She had to say something. 'My parents were happy most of the time, though finding enough funds to live on was always an issue for them.'

She shrugged. 'When I entered the workforce I studied hard and ensured my savings were adequate. My ex-husband was a doctor, although not a thrifty one, and it's taken me several months to climb out of the debt he left me with, but I finally managed it. I am a woman determined to find myself secure.'

'A sensible person?' He tilted his head at her. 'I don't think I know any thrifty women.'

'Poor you.' Dryly. She tilted her own head. 'I am prudent.' She thought about what she'd done with him and added, 'Mostly.' She'd told him too much. Though Jen had always said her relationship with her ex had been one-sided. She'd saved, he'd spent. She'd cared for him more than he'd cared for her. She wouldn't be doing that again, ever. 'Enough about me, tell me more about your grandmother.'

'Taste the wine.'

She inhaled the fruity aroma of the wine and then took a sip. 'Very nice. About your grandmother?'

He sat back and gave her one of those half amused, half warning glances. 'When my grandfather died many years ago, my grandmother took over the family empire until she could hand it on to her three sons. She has had much grief in her life and far too many deaths. Now there is only me, Sofia and Isabella left. And lots of distant cousins like Diego.'

Ah, so Diego was a distant cousin of his. She wondered if Jen knew that. Cleo could quite believe it was an empire judging by the wealth that surrounded Felipe and Luisa.

Felipe went on. 'Before he died, my father managed his and Sofia's part of the business and I managed my grandmother's and my own. She was an astute businesswoman and very used to making decisions for the family. It was her contacts who first discovered Sofia was in trouble. Her fingers are in many pies.'

He glanced with affection and obvious respect towards Doña Luisa. 'For the last ten years I have been telling her it is time for her to sit back and savour the time she has left.'

'I'm sorry. I can see she is unwell. You said you would care for her.' That night. 'Will she move back in with you when she needs more care?'

'She has refused. Though, as I said before, we have thankfully completed the new oncology hospice that she has consented to consider when she requires twenty-four-hour care.'

'We have completed', as in just his family, or 'we' as in Barcelona has completed? she wondered. She strongly suspected the former.

He shrugged. 'Though I would prefer she stayed in her own apartments with full assistance but that is up to her.'

She remembered their discussion about oncologists. 'And this is the building, the new centre you spoke about before? Where you work?'

'Sí.'

Felipe's phone buzzed quietly in his pocket and he excused himself to walk to a window. A rapid one-sided conversation and then he moved across to his grandmother. 'Àvia, there is something I must attend to at the hospice. I will be no more than an hour. Can you stay from your bed that long?'

'I am not dead yet, Felipe. Go. Take your midwife. She would be more interested in your building there than sitting in a corner, watching us talk. Show her your pride and joy.'

The frown he sent his grandmother made Cleo cringe with embarrassment. He didn't want to take her.

But he said, 'Would you like to see the new hospice, Cleo?'

And she could say nothing except, 'If you are sure that will be acceptable.'

His astonished look said it all. 'Who would complain?'

She laughed at his arrogance. She probably shouldn't. She was in his sandpit now. But she couldn't help herself. She had nothing but her courage to shield her. 'I'm sure no one would dare,' she said, her voice dry.

He raised his brows but his eyes smiled. He shook his head but didn't comment. They rode down in the elevator, and when they emerged she had to skip a little to keep up, but he didn't seem to notice. He was on a mission. Typical.

His usual driver waited with the car, and she wondered if he'd had warning or just…always waited around until he was needed.

The driver opened the rear door for her and she wondered again whether to slide across or just sit and make Felipe go to the other side of the car, but he was always there before she could make a decision.

Then she thought of all the aristocratic women she'd ever watched on TV and none of them had ever slid across a back seat. So she assumed Felipe expected her to stay put.

Good to get that sorted in her head.

Too many unknown areas with the weight of such a long, distinguished family history and the ridiculous wealth that surrounded these people.

She looked forward to being home in her own humble yet comfortable environment.

'Where is the hospice?' she asked as the car pulled away from the kerb.

'Ten minutes from here. One of my patients is asking for me. He is a very dear friend of mine and I would never ignore any request he made.'

As a lead oncologist he must have many other demands on his time. 'It must have been difficult for you to get away for the week to go to Australia.'

'Yes. Though nobody is irreplaceable. My departure created yet more work for those who had no need to expand their duties. Sometimes Doña Luisa forgets how busy I am, but in this case she was right to send me instead of anyone else.'

So, he hadn't chosen to retrieve Sofia. She could see how much he cared for his grandmother and she wasn't surprised he had gone. She'd already decided he wasn't the ogre Sofia proclaimed so loudly.

'I am constantly looking for the right staff for the hospice.' He turned in his seat to give her his full attention. 'Why are you wasting time shuttling people in aircraft between countries? Your kindness would fit well in my field.'

His comment warmed her. And confused her. How had he come to that conclusion in their short acquaintance? Yes, she wanted to hear more about his work; she wanted to hear anything except that there was no future for them. She needed to banish those ridiculous thoughts.

'As you said, there is a similarity between the care of those at the beginning and the end of life. It is interesting you say that because I had thought about doing oncology nursing when I first moved from midwifery.'

'*Sí.* I could imagine you there.' He tilted his head to study her. 'I could see you as one who stands at the gate and comforts those going and those who must bid them goodbye.'

'I've had no experience with that.'

'I'm not sure if you understand my hospice. It is not only for the old and infirm. It is for all ages, all terminal souls, from infant to child to adult to elder as they leave their families. It's about simple beauty and peaceful surroundings to pass from this world into the next.'

She frowned. Did he mean euthanasia? Her face must have registered the question.

'Not like a certain clinic in Switzerland but a place of quiet, comfort and solace for nature to take its course. With excellent support. But I do need someone who could impart the secrets of the midwife to those who think efficiency is the same thing.'

There was a thread of frustration in his voice. 'Someone who can fulfil the needs of others and work to make that happen without cold competence and too little understanding. Most of my staff are wonderful but some need more guidance in compassion.'

The car pulled up in front of a large white building with tall standard roses in ceramic pots that stood like soldiers on both sides of the path to make a floral corridor. Marble steps, as well as a ramp to the side, led to the oval doorway and the automatic doors. A discreet sign read 'Hospicio Luisa'. Named after his grandmother, he'd said. Of course.

Inside the doors, warm brown mosaics on the floor and artistic silver branches adorned the eggshell-blue walls like a tree growing from the doorway and curving away on the left towards some elevators.

A glowing parquetry desk with soft pale blue leather chairs sat in front in welcome and to the right a fountain tinkled beside two stunning life-size statues of angels. Flowers scented the air and created a foyer less like a medical facility and more like an elegant apartment block lobby for the rich and famous.

The woman at the desk smiled and inclined her head respectfully at Felipe. She looked curiously at Cleo.

'Good morning, Elisheba,' he said. 'Please ask the nursing supervisor on duty to meet me in Raymond's apartment.'

The woman nodded. '*Sí*, Don Felipe.' Her respect was coloured by her warmth towards him and Cleo could see her delight in seeing him. Curiouser and curiouser. A different side again to this multifaceted man, and he intrigued her even more. She had seen the Spanish lover, the autocratic head of the family, the caring grandson and now the respected professional doctor.

Felipe directed her to a pair of white elevators and they rose to the third floor.

When they came out again there was more warm brown flooring, pale green walls of early summer, and flowers.

Every time they passed staff the response was the same delight as the woman from downstairs had shown. Felipe knew all their first names and enquired occasionally about family members. From the warmth of those who hailed him, he was a much-admired and looked-up-to doctor.

Unlike the rich and famous Felipe, this person she could relate to. She thought of the conversation in the car on the way here. There was definitely something they had in common. A passion for their work in helping others.

She stood beside him as they passed many rooms, all different pastel colours with plush chairs and large windows, and he paused frequently to share a particular vantage point, or luxury fitting, or pleasing colour scheme with her, and she saw and couldn't help but appreciate his fierce dedication and passion for his hospice.

At the end of the long corridor he knocked on a partially closed door.

A name on the door read, 'Don Raymond Ruiz'. The faint voice of a man bade them enter.

Two sides of the room held large windows that overlooked the cityscape and on the third wall hung a glorious print of a rainforest beside a door that she assumed led to the bathroom. In the corner was a small kitchenette and a bar fridge was tucked away.

The man in the bed looked gaunt and very pale, but of an age with Felipe, terminally ill well before his time. Yet despite his obvious frailty, his eyes danced with amusement and interest at seeing Felipe with Cleo.

'Who is this you have brought to meet me, my friend?' The educated accent was similar to Felipe's and his English as impeccable as her escort's.

Felipe crossed the room and took the man's skeletal hand in his. 'Raymond. You summoned me.' He smiled warmly at him. 'This is Cleo Wren. A midwife and nurse from Australia, and companion to my cousin Sofia who has just returned from Sydney with her new babe.'

'A pleasure to meet you, Cleo.' He looked from one to the other and his eyes shone with mischief. Cleo liked him immediately. He certainly wasn't awed by Felipe.

'A pleasure to meet you, too, Don Raymond.'

'Raymond.'

There was a knock at the door and a tall calm-faced woman around Cleo's age came in. She nodded at Mr Ruiz. 'Don Raymond. Don Felipe?'

'Thank you for your call, Maya. This is Sister Cleo Wren from Australia. I would appreciate if you offer her a tour of our facility while I speak to Raymond.'

The woman smiled at Cleo. 'With pleasure. We are very proud of the hospice.' She turned to Felipe. 'How long would you like us to be?'

Felipe glanced at his friend, who flashed ten fingers at him. 'A quarter of an hour would be sufficient for a brief showing.'

He looked at Cleo. 'I would like your opinions on the facility, please, Cleo.'

She nodded and went with her minder out the door, secretly delighted to have the chance to explore Felipe's world and not intrude on what was obviously a private and important conversation.

By the time Cleo returned with Maya fifteen minutes later, she'd learned several things.

First, that Felipe was held in awe by the staff. When she'd questioned Maya on the reason it had come across as his determination to overcome all obstacles and his single-minded dedication to create this peaceful world for those at the end of their lives.

She'd also discovered that a lot of the capital expenditure had been donated by Felipe, but more importantly Felipe made himself available day and night for the patients and the staff. The relatives, he saw through the day.

As they traversed two more floors, the hospice itself continued to amaze and delight Cleo with the calm colours, soft furnishings and attention to tiny details, like curtains, bed lights and nurse call, which could be managed by voice technology or buttons by the bed.

Each room held a tiny kitchenette and the actual kitchen downstairs was available for the staff, visitors and, of course, the patients, and served delicious and nutritious snacks and meals twenty-four hours a day. All could be summoned by a push of the bell.

Towards the end of the tour Cleo couldn't help asking a more direct question. 'Is it very expensive for the patients?'

Maya laughed. 'It depends. To spend your last days here would cost the same as the public hospital for those who cannot afford to pay, and is very, very expensive for those who can,' Maya said with mischief. 'The idea is to have both kinds of clientele in residence.'

'And do you have enough staff?'

'*Sí.* Almost. It is an excellent place to work but the interviews are thorough for those who wish to work here. We are looking for a certain type of person.'

Cleo guessed that was the royal 'we' and it

was Felipe who was looking for a certain type of nurse and doctor. He'd said as much in the car on the way here.

Maya went on. 'We have only a short time to care for these souls, but it is one of the most important times of their lives.' Her sincerity was obvious, and Cleo nodded her head. It was how she felt about midwifery.

'I totally agree. Thank you so much for showing me around.'

'It is rare that I have the chance.' The curiosity in the other woman's eyes made Cleo smile but what could she say? His grandmother made me come? She didn't think so.

When they arrived back at the room Felipe held Raymond's shoulder with a firm grip as their gazes held. Felipe dropped his hand. 'Goodbye, my friend.'

'And you, Felipe,' Raymond said. 'Find happiness.'

Cleo hung back at the charged atmosphere and Maya looked sad for a moment as she observed the two men. She waited quietly until she had Felipe's attention. 'Is there anything else you wish me to do?'

'Keep me updated.' Felipe's eyes were shadowed and Cleo wanted to take his arm and offer support. His friend was clearly dying, though apparently with a calmness and serenity Cleo had rarely seen.

'Cleo?' Raymond's tired voice held amusement. She turned and smiled at him. He beckoned so she went across to the bed and leaned down. 'Make my friend smile,' he whispered.

Cleo nodded. Kissed the pale, dry cheek gently. Said very softly, so nobody else could hear, 'Someone needs to not take him so seriously.' But she had learned that others deeply appreciated Felipe Gonzales and now more than ever she wanted to know more about the man she could see. But then he would be so much harder to resist.

Raymond relaxed back in the bed and closed his eyes. But his lips curved in a smile. Cleo stepped away from the bed and found Felipe beside her. He took her arm. 'We need to get back.'

Maya had gone, and when they left, the sleeping man was alone in the room. She wasn't sure if it was a trick of light but there seemed to be sunshine playing on the path through the rainforest picture and the room held a golden glow.

When the car drew away from the hospice Felipe turned his face to the window. She touched his arm, the expression in his eyes showing for a moment his distress, but it shuttered as he looked her way.

'What did you think of my clinic?' He gestured back the way they'd come.

'I thought it was beautiful. Perfect for the care of those who need comfort and tranquillity.'

'Yes. It is satisfying to see the dream become a reality.'

'Your staff are rightly very proud of the service offered. And of you.'

He waved his hand as if discounting that. His mouth tightened.

'Don't wave it away.' She remembered his grandmother's words. How she wanted him to take time for his own happiness. 'They love you. You obviously deserve their respect and appreciation.' When he didn't answer she said, 'I'm sorry that your friend Raymond is so unwell.' She wanted to add, *He's far too young to die, but when was age a barrier to loss of life?* 'He told me to make you smile.'

He looked up. Shook his head. And his expression softened as he smiled. For a moment he wasn't the far more reserved man she was seeing so much of in Spain.

'Ah, there he is,' she teased softly, suddenly desperate to do as Raymond had asked her. Felipe, the less austere Felipe, reacted to her tone, relaxing a fraction more, the smile still playing around his wicked mouth. She wondered which facet of this fascinating man was more real. The dancer, the doctor or the Don?

'There is who, Cleo?' His voice was low and sexy.

His eyes were dark, and dangerous, and he leaned her way. She was mad but she said it anyway. For the smile she'd promised, she told herself. 'The flamenco dancer.'

His smile widened and he reached long fingers across and captured her hand in his. He already held her gaze. Drew her wrist slowly to his mouth until his lips bowed and he kissed her sensitive skin, making her shiver with the long, leisurely promise. 'I could certainly show you that man.'

The car stopped. They'd arrived. *Oh, my goodness*, she thought, and with difficulty dragged her eyes away from his to look at the escape hatch.

When they arrived back at Doña Luisa's house Cleo had to fight to clear the fog that particular version of Felipe had created in her mind. They had arrived just in time for the meal.

'Come,' Doña Luisa called out. 'We go through for tapas.'

Tapas was a good thing. An excellent diversion from the swirl of emotion she'd been left with from the hospice. And most definitely from the volcanic reaction she'd unleashed in Felipe in the car.

That Felipe, Sofia's cousin, wanted comfort, safety and peace for others, which was clear at the hospice named after his grandmother, Cleo had no doubt now that he wanted the best for his cousin, too.

She needed time to think, some distance between herself and Felipe, for her fluctuating emotions to settle down. She needed to concentrate on the job and not think so much about the powerful, seductive man beside her.

While they had been away rapport had been renewed between Sofia and Doña Luisa because the younger woman was smiling as she helped her grandmother to her feet. A pram, possibly one almost as old as their hostess, had appeared, and Isabella reposed quietly amidst its ancient splendour.

CHAPTER FOURTEEN

FELIPE LIFTED HIS hand towards the small of her back to usher her through to the dining room but she skipped ahead like a frightened doe. He allowed his hand to fall again and smiled. He'd liked that glimpse of a different Cleo. The one he'd met in the flamenco club and who had been markedly absent ever since they'd met again in Sofia's hospital room.

She walked swiftly to increase the distance between them and though they entered the dining room together they moved apart like ripples on a pond. He turned to assist his grandmother into her chair.

Cleo went to stand beside Sofia.

His grandmother touched his hand and inclined her head. 'You watch her. Always. I see your eyes.' Said very quietly as she shot him a wicked grin. 'I thought you didn't like Australians?'

He frowned at her and lifted his head to see if Cleo had heard the word *Australians*. She was talking to Sofia and they were both admiring the pram.

'Enough, Àvia, you tease me. She is help for Sofia.'

'Is she? No attraction there?' A quirk of white eyebrows. 'There is nothing between you at all?' She made a derisive sound. 'I have eyes.'

He turned his shocked gaze to her, sincerely hoping she was talking about her own eyes and not others who might have been watching him in Australia. 'You are mistaken.'

'Me?' She laughed and then coughed and turned pale enough to worry him. But slowly the colour crept back into her cheeks.

'You are changed since you came back.' Said a little breathlessly. 'I will find out why.' Short sentences. 'Then.' A breath. 'We will discuss it.' His grandmother composed herself into her chair and called to Sofia. Patted the seat beside her.

There was nothing to discuss. But his grandmother's seating arrangements left him to sit next to Cleo. What was his *àvia* playing at?

Thankfully the food arrived, so he could pretend to divert his attention to the array of small dishes that circled the middle of the table.

But his grandmother's words swirled in his head. She could see his intense attraction to Cleo. Why would he be so surprised? His grandmother's passion had always been watching others.

Of course she'd seen. Next she'd be investigating Cleo from her deathbed.

This wasn't good. He had no doubt Cleo would be unimpressed as well.

He looked across at his cousin. Another accurate observation by his grandmother. In this instance he was thankful she'd uncovered it and still felt guilty as hell that he'd allowed Sofia to slip unnoticed into a disaster. He should have checked on her himself as soon as his father had died.

And in an indirect way his grandmother's meddling in her grandchildren's lives had also brought him to having the woman he could not ignore beside him. A woman who had infiltrated his senses like the subtle scent she wore. Aware of every move of her arm. Every turn of her head. The way Raymond, and even Maya, had tacitly given a nod of approval for the woman he had brought with him to the hospice.

He saw all the good in Cleo, but he had to keep her at arm's length for now because he had enough on his plate without starting a torrid affair with someone who was going to fly back to Australia in two weeks. And it *would* be torrid if their one night together was any indication.

There were several minutes of silence as delicacies were eaten, though throughout his meal his awareness increased that neither his grandmother nor Cleo was eating very much.

He turned to study Cleo's plate and asked quietly, 'Is the food not to your liking?'

'It's wonderful.' A crease lay between her brows. 'Though I'm afraid I don't know what half of the things are.'

He pointed with his finger. 'Green peppers.'

'Not chillies, then. I'm so pleased. They smell amazing but I was afraid to be mistaken.' She smiled and took one with the fork provided.

'*Sí.* Tiny green peppers, not chilli peppers. They are roasted soft, flavoursome, and that touch of coconut is very tasty.'

He watched her face as she tried the different dishes, eating slowly. Savouring. Concentrating. Serious. As if learning the tastes. Cataloguing. She made him smile. There was nothing wrong with just enjoying her company while she was here.

He would really like to see her laugh again, like they had that one night in Australia.

'Where does the word *tapas* come from?' Cleo asked.

It was as if she needed to understand everything with her curiosity. She made him curious as to why she was like that. '*Tapas* is the word for a lid.' He gestured with his hand so she understood. 'A small empty plate that the barman would put on top of the beer glass to stop flies from landing on the rim of the glass.'

He leaned towards her. 'They say that one day,

a barman put a piece of meat on top of the empty plate, to eat with the beer, which the patrons enjoyed.'

He shrugged. 'The story goes that then different things were placed on the plate on top of the glass and so a sophisticated tapas culture grew in Spain.' He spread his hands. 'The best is in Barcelona.'

She laughed and he congratulated himself just a little smugly on drawing her out.

'You think Barcelona has the best of everything.'

'Of course.'

She shook her head. 'So, what are those?' she asked, pointing at a dish.

'That is my favourite. Cured duck breast with fresh figs, rosemary and honey.'

She looked intrigued. He pointed.

'That is Iberian pork fillet with pears.' A wave of his hand towards the shellfish. 'You must recognise the oysters.'

She nodded. 'The Iberian coast surrounds you, so seafood should play a strong part in your tapas menus.'

A sudden loud squealing of tyres followed by a crash from the street below made Felipe hurriedly rise from his chair, muttering, 'Excuse me.' He crossed to the window to pull back the curtains. His grandmother's usually peaceful street lay in chaos. Tables and chairs from the footpath outside the café on the corner had been flung around and a car was buried nose first in the doorway of the café.

Alba appeared beside him. He turned to her. 'Call the police and the ambulance. I will go down to see if I can help.'

Cleo appeared at his shoulder. 'I'll come with you.'

His first instinct was to decline, to protect her from the chaos below, but of course she was a trained nurse with valuable medical skills. He would need help until the emergency services arrived and together they had the skills to benefit any accident victim.

And she was calm. It seemed to him that she was always calm. 'Thank you.'

When they reached the lift it had returned to the ground floor and he cursed. It was not a fast lift. 'Let us take the stairs.'

She nodded with instant agreement and he glanced at her shoes, which were low-heeled and sensible. *Sensible like her*, he thought, and after the pampered women he'd been exposed to for so many years he knew why that drew him so much.

On the ground floor, they crossed the street and saw a small crowd had gathered and voices were being raised.

Felipe pushed through them with Cleo behind him. 'I am a doctor,' he said. 'Was anyone on the chairs?' Perhaps under the car? 'Has anyone been hurt apart from the people in the car?'

'No, a woman and man. In the car,' someone offered.

Thank God the chairs had been empty, Felipe thought. He crossed himself because earlier there had been children there. Steam rose from the fractured radiator of the car but despite the loudness of the impact it didn't look too bad.

A man stumbled from the driver's side of the car and almost made it to the passenger side before he crumpled to the ground groaning and holding his head. Blood trickled down his face beneath his fingers.

Felipe moved towards him and turned to Cleo. 'There is a woman in the car. I think perhaps she is in need of a midwife.'

'No, no, no.' The woman's cries could be heard more clearly now. 'The baby is coming.' No doubt about the cry this time.

He opened the passenger door and spoke gently to the labouring woman. 'Are you hurt? Apart from being in labour?'

The woman settled briefly as her contraction eased. 'No. I am not hurt.'

'I am a doctor and I will be with you shortly. This woman she is *llevadora*—a midwife. I must help your husband.'

The woman struggled to get out of the car to see to her husband then leaned back in her seat, sobbing. '*Idiota!* He drove too fast when I said the baby was coming.'

Felipe turned. Where was Cleo?

'*Soy enfermera,*' he heard her say quietly. I am a nurse. The onlookers parted.

The younger woman's frantic gaze latched onto Cleo and something she saw in Cleo's calm gaze seemed to allow her some relief.

CHAPTER FIFTEEN

CLEO ARRIVED BESIDE the car at the same time as the next contraction caught the woman. She moaned and pushed at the same time.

Cleo had no doubt birth was imminent, which she considered a good thing after an accident like this.

Trauma to the uterus and/or rapid deceleration could be silently dangerous for pregnancy. The placenta could shear from the wall of the uterus and cut off the blood supply to the baby. Or the mother could bleed badly and yet feel no pain. No, she wasn't going there. They would have a healthy baby born.

'Are you hurt?'

The woman held her stomach, glanced down at it, but shook her head. She glared in the direction of her husband. *'Idiota!'* she said again, and then sighed. 'I hope he is not badly hurt.'

'Perhaps just a little bit hurt,' Cleo said, and suppressed a smile.

The woman shook her head but she smiled.

Until the next contraction and the woman bore down again. She heard the small grunt and Cleo looked for a place to ease the birth.

She met the woman's eyes and gestured to the road. 'Can you move out of the car?' she asked, thinking giving birth might be awkward in the car.

The woman shook her head. Cleo didn't want to move her either, really, in case something else was hurt. It was unlikely, but the impact hadn't been near the fuel tank and she had no doubt if they needed to exit the area swiftly Felipe would tell them so in no uncertain terms.

The woman grunted again.

Cleo pulled the husband's jacket from beside her feet onto the road and knelt on it. 'I'll try to push the seat back, but can you help me do that?' She gestured to help explain what she meant.

Cleo leaned down to push the small bar under the seat and the woman gave a small jerk with her body backwards and thankfully the seat slid easily and created some room in front of the woman, except for a large, soft overnight case jammed next to her feet.

It would have to be enough. Felipe was busy with the bleeding man, who appeared to have a shoulder injury as well. The woman leaned forward with her hands on her knees and breathed.

Cleo had nothing to wash her hands with, no gloves, no towels. But they had a conscious and alert mother. It could have been worse. The woman could slide forward to the edge of the seat. That would work. She was more worried the baby would be compromised than she was about the awkwardness of the actual birth, but she had Felipe there, too. Hopefully, soon emergency medical help would arrive. 'I am Cleo. What is your name?'

'Elena.' A downward grunt of late labour. 'Not how I was supposed to have my baby.'

'No.' Cleo smiled warmly. 'Is this your first?'

'No. Third.' An experienced mother, then. A bonus.

They could do this together. 'Elena,' she said slowly, 'some babies are impatient. Yours is one such. May I put your bag behind you to lean against so you can sit forward at the edge of the seat? To make room for the birth?'

Elena grunted again and Cleo squeezed the bag out of the small space while Elena shuffled forward on the seat.

Felipe edged in quietly beside her. 'I'll push it in while you help her stay forward.' With relief she nodded, and he spoke quietly to Elena while they both helped her move forward and he pushed the bulky bag down with the other hand until the woman sat perched at the edge of the seat with the bag supporting her back.

'Like a birthing stool,' Cleo said with a slight smile.

Elena grimaced. 'Though it is better.'

Cleo touched Elena's arm gently. 'If you have your baby here now, I believe all will be well. Then the ambulance will come and take you all to the hospital.'

Elena said something too fast to understand but Cleo didn't need all the words. She understood the word 'idiot' again and had the feeling Elena's husband was in serious trouble with his wife! But first the baby.

'It will be soon.' She spoke calmly. 'Can you lift up so I can remove your underwear? Pantaloons?' She hoped that was the right word. The contraction had eased but Elena was panting, her eyes glued to Cleo's. She nodded quickly and reached up to the small handgrip above her head and lifted her bottom.

With a discreet shuffle under the voluminous skirt Cleo managed to hook the pair of knickers and slide them down Elena's legs. She left one side on at the ankle.

Felipe said beside her, 'I have phoned Alba to send down some washcloths and towels.'

'And my handbag.' She did have handwash in there, but it would be too late to use it before the birth. And one pack of gloves. But there was a twin pack of small plastic disposable cord clamps because she never knew which country she'd end up in or when a baby would decide to come. Not that she had scissors to cut the cord with. 'And scissors.' Though perhaps she'd wrap the placenta for the hospital to separate it from the baby later.

She asked Elena for the scarf she had around her neck. 'For the baby.' Elena stared and then nodded and tore the colourful cashmere scarf off her throat.

Felipe spoke rapidly into his phone and the two women settled themselves more comfortably. The scarf was handed to Cleo. She heard Felipe behind her instructing the crowd to turn their backs and form a circle to give privacy to the two women.

Elena's face contorted and as her breaths were expelled she said loudly, 'The baby is coming.'

Cleo discreetly lifted her skirts. She couldn't help the smile that grew at the sight of the dark bulge of the baby's head. The mother was always right.

She nodded calmly. '*Sí.* Your baby is coming. All is good.'

Felipe murmured beside her and Elena nodded sharply and gripped the edge of the seat. The sound of a mother bearing down became unmistakable in the silence of the small space.

A gush.

A splash as more waters escaped. Poor car.

The birth of the head and then a tumble of damp limbs. It was over very quickly.

The rush of a tiny body into Cleo's waiting

hands, which were suddenly heavy, though the baby lay still in a frozen moment after birth.

But there was tone in the small limbs. Rapid birth would cause a baby some shock. And was to be expected under the circumstances.

'He is stunned. Give him a moment.' Calmly Cleo leaned forward with the scarf and brushed it over the baby, wiping it firmly in long strokes. She crooned to it. 'Nice big breath, baby. You can do it.'

The limbs tensed, pale eyelids quivered and blinked, and his neck stiffened.

The newborn coughed and first a weak cry broke the silence and then a louder one. His eyes opened in round surprise.

Cleo heard the sudden expulsion of breath behind her as Felipe exhaled in relief. She heard the mother's gasp as she reached for her baby, and the murmurings from the small crowd that had gathered, though after one quick glare from Felipe they didn't turn around to look.

In the distance she heard the wail of an ambulance. But the sound of the escalating baby's cries was the best of all sounds.

'You are very clever, Elena,' Cleo said to the mother as she lifted the other woman's blouse to expose the skin of her soft abdomen and laid the still-connected baby across her warm belly.

The umbilical cord was short and unless she

cut it, Cleo couldn't lift the baby higher onto his mother's chest.

Felipe murmured in Spanish and the amusement in his voice was tinged with relief.

The father had crawled to where they were, inside the circle of turned backs, and leaned his head against the door of the car.

Alba pushed through the onlookers with towels and Cleo's handbag.

'Mare de Déus!' she exclaimed at the scene. And dropped the towels beside Cleo and waved the handbag uncertainly.

Cleo turned to Felipe. 'My hands are no use like this.' They were wet and bloody, though she'd wiped them on the scarf when she'd dried the baby.

Now she reached for a clean towel and wiped the part of the baby she could get to. She laid another fresh towel across the infant and mother to keep them warm.

She turned her face Felipe's way. 'There's a small black purse in the zipped compartment at the back of the bag. Can you open it and remove the cord clamps, please?'

He shook his head in disbelief. Said something to the new mother. Cleo didn't bother translating, and Elena and her husband laughed weakly through their tears. The husband stared in awe at the baby then with immense gratitude at Cleo.

'What did you say?' Cleo asked Felipe.

'I said how many people do we know who carry such things as these in their handbags?' He held up the see-through sterile packet of two blue plastic cord clamps.

'And they're even the right colour,' Cleo said matter-of-factly. Elena moaned in surprise as an unexpected contraction rolled over her and Cleo soothed her, murmured about the afterbirth and a short time later bundled up the placenta in one of the towels and tucked it next to the baby.

When all was done, she felt the mother's belly, and thanked her lucky stars that the rock-hard uterus she felt beneath her hands was contracting and healthy. They didn't need to battle a haemorrhage as well as a birth in the front seat of a small vehicle.

Felipe tore open the sterile packet so she could reach over and take out one of the cord clamps.

She eased baby away from mother for a moment so she could see the infant's belly, clicked the little clamp shut over the thick cord an inch above the baby's skin and the next clamp half an inch further towards the mother's end of the cord.

'I don't have scissors, but the ambulance will. I didn't need the clamps if I'm not cutting the cord but it's safer to do it in case someone accidentally stretches the cord and it breaks or the placenta somehow ends up below the baby. I've seen a baby's blood volume compromised like that before.'

Felipe stared at her. Then shook his head.

Cleo narrowed her eyes. 'What?'

'Nothing.'

CHAPTER SIXTEEN

FELIPE COULD NOT help but stare at her. This woman he had left on Sunday morning, mere days ago, who had reappeared in his life like a breath of fresh air. She knelt on the road, smiling at a stranger. As calm as if Elena had just given birth in a labour ward suite.

'I'm looking at you. So composed. Matter-of-fact about this moment.' He shook his head. 'I have seen many births as a student doctor but none as reassuring as this emergency with no one for back-up.'

She smiled at him. Her face was softer than he'd ever seen, as if she were totally content with her world.

Inside himself something shifted. A fracture of time, a blending of past and present, so that at this moment he remembered the velvet of her skin beneath his hands and yet could study now the curve of her cheek as she bent over the mother and murmured to her.

The scent of new baby and blood, burnt rubber

and the press of bodies was in his nostrils, and yet there was a lightness to the moment he could not believe. She was amazing. Something else shifted. The urge to fight for her, to rise above the obstacles lying between them, stirred in his chest. Was there any possibility of a future with this woman? Because he wanted her for his own.

His hand clenched. He had wronged Cleo when he had walked away from her without giving them a chance. He remembered the generous giving of her lovemaking, her full attention when he had been speaking of his past, how incredible their connection had been. But he'd still walked away.

She broke into his thoughts softly. 'I had you here for back-up.'

'Sí.' In this instance. He hoped he would have been of use if needed, but once before he had been unsuccessful when attending childbirth. He winced as a painful memory suddenly returned to haunt him. One that had changed the course of his work because briefly, years ago as a student doctor, he, too, had considered working with mothers and babies.

He'd tried to resuscitate an infant he'd helped to birth but it had not gone well and the baby had died. No matter that later the autopsy had proved the baby had lacked a functioning heart. The trauma of it had been enough for him to know that the life and death stakes of working with newborns in Obstetrics was not for him.

His Cleo had stepped up and taken the braver path. He had taken the path of caring for people at the other end of life—when no one expected miracles. But that was good, too, because it was his passion now and all was as it should be.

His brow furrowed. He hadn't thought of that infant in years. He hadn't thought of a lot of the things that now dominated his mind when he was around this woman.

Enough. Later. 'Here comes the ambulance.' She did not understand just how extraordinary she was. He was realising again how much that intrigued him.

The ambulance wailed to a stop with the onlookers now standing back, and very swiftly Elena and her baby were safely bundled inside the large vehicle.

Cleo's hands had been disinfected thanks to the ambulance personnel, though her cream dress had marks that would not be so easily cleaned.

When the ambulance pulled away, a muttering Alba had bundled the remaining washcloths and towels into a black disposable bag and marched them straight to the rubbish bin. As they rode up together in the lift, Felipe saw Alba steal glances at Cleo as if she couldn't decide if she were a good woman or a disaster waiting to happen.

His midwife had her eyes shut and a gentle

smile on her face as she leaned back against the wall of the elevator. He watched the gentle rise and fall of her breasts and skimmed the vivid red marks on her dress and shook his head again.

Alba spoke tightly. 'I will find her a gown to wear while I try to save that dress and she washes.'

Felipe considered her ire. Knew it wasn't aimed at Cleo but against people who imposed on guests of his grandmother by bleeding on them.

Cleo opened her eyes. 'Thank you.'

He recalled her speaking to Elena and realised she actually spoke his language quite well, and he wondered why he hadn't noticed that before. There must be a story in that, too. It was surprising how badly he wanted to know all her stories. 'We will return to my villa as soon as you've washed. Grandmother will understand.'

He watched her consider the marks on her dress and the spots of blood on her legs. 'Perhaps that's a good idea.' Another rueful scan. 'Before I touch anything or anyone.'

All would be forgiven, he thought, after such heroics, but held his peace. Maybe he was making too much of this. Her actions were, after all, those of any woman with her medical experience.

But he knew the changes inside him, the ones his grandmother had seen, had shifted yet again.

Had he always held himself back from meaningful relationships? Been cool and aloof until finally he had found someone who had broken through that shell and shaken him badly, like Cleo was shaking him to the core now?

He thought of the couple downstairs, their new baby arriving with such drama but, thankfully, safely. That had also shaken him.

He wasn't like his own father, who'd had trouble connecting with any other human being. He was a good man, could be a good husband and—dared he think it?—could also be a good father one day…

The lift doors opened and Alba hustled Cleo away.

He took himself to the nearest bathroom to wash his own hands and ensure he was presentable before he returned to his grandmother, whom he knew would be avid for news.

He remained pensive.

His grandmother eyed him shrewdly. 'You look shocked. Is the woman well?'

'Mother and infant are well. You have had a baby born in your street.'

'Not the first. Better than a stable, I imagine.'

'Indeed.' He smiled at his grandmother. 'Does anything faze you?'

Old eyes twinkled. 'The way you look at the midwife.'

'Really.' He could believe that. Little escaped his grandmother's eye but now she'd see even more. He didn't comment further but it was something he would have to think about soon. 'Where is Sofia?'

'She has gone to refresh the baby in the guest room.'

'With your permission we will take our leave when she returns. Cleo has a need to change her clothes after her heroics downstairs.'

His grandmother sat back and raised her brows. 'Her heroics? Aren't you the doctor?'

He smiled. 'The mother was giving birth, not undergoing chemotherapy. That's never been my speciality.'

She waved a veined hand. 'In my day, the doctor did everything.' Then she leaned forward. 'Are your emotions truly engaged with this woman?'

'She is Sofia's midwife,' he said evasively.

'That was not what I asked. Have you finally allowed someone to become close to you?'

Footsteps and the topic of their conversation appeared at the door just in time. 'Ah, Cleo. Come in. I was just telling my grandmother how lucky we were to have you here for the birth.'

CHAPTER SEVENTEEN

CLEO STOPPED AT the door, aware of the raised tension in the room. She'd heard the word for midwife. And she looked a mess. Both occupants were immaculate as they waited for her to enter. She did, slowly, and stopped short of the chair where Doña Luisa sat.

'We were fortunate everything turned out well for all involved.' She looked at Doña Luisa. 'My apologies for my appearance. Alba has been very kind to sponge my dress but I'm afraid…' She trailed off.

Doña Luisa waved that away. 'No need for apologies. Felipe has already been singing your praises.' The older lady's eyes were fixed on Cleo as if looking for something she couldn't quite see.

Sofia returned then, pushing the pram and a sleeping baby, and if Cleo wasn't mistaken it seemed Felipe was very happy at her arrival.

'On that note we will take our leave to return another time,' he said.

Doña Luisa raised her brows but she did look

tired. 'Send Sofia to me tomorrow. In the morning, and she may stay with me until siesta.' She glanced at Felipe. 'You and Cleo may return for dinner tomorrow night if I am well enough.'

There was something going on here that Cleo couldn't grasp. Byplay she didn't understand, and that seemed to include her, between grandmother and grandson that hadn't been evident when they had first arrived. Had she caused that? She hoped not and kept quiet.

Sofia kissed her grandmother's cheek and lifted the baby from the pram. Doña Luisa's face softened as she glanced down at the sleeping infant.

She murmured, 'She is beautiful, like her mother.'

Sofia smiled and said, 'We will see you tomorrow.'

Going back in the car, Sofia seemed pensive. Finally she said quietly, 'She is definitely dying?'

'Yes.' Felipe spoke softly as well, and his sadness underlay the single word. 'But on her terms. She tells me her life has been well lived. And too long, apparently.'

'Is there anything else you can do for her?' Sofia wiped a tear from her cheek.

'She is done with the treatment and now it is time to keep her comfortable. I watch her closely.' Felipe gently touched his cousin's hand.

Sofia lifted her chin. 'I apologise for being difficult when you first found me. She said she asked you to come for me. That she was the one who found out about Terence taking my money.'

Felipe smiled gently at her and Cleo wanted to cheer for his kindness. '*Sí.* But if I had known the extent of his crimes, she would not have needed to ask me. I would have come anyway.'

'I understand.' She looked at Cleo. 'Perhaps my cousin is not quite as horrid as his father was.'

Cleo felt the humour of the situation. And let her eyes travel over the two dark heads, and their identical stubborn chins. She said to both Sofia and Felipe, 'I'm glad for you. If your family can help when somebody lets you down, that is better. And even less reason for me to be here if Sofia is going to be spending more time with her grandmother.'

Maybe she could get away earlier than two weeks, which would be a very sensible thing to do.

Sofia leaned forward and touched Cleo's knee. 'Do not think you can go yet.' A fierce look at her cousin under black brows. 'I don't trust him completely.' But it was said playfully.

'Why not? What can he do? You have your own house.'

This time it was Felipe who laughed, out loud, until his shoulders shook. Sofia stared at her cousin in amazement. 'I had no idea you could do that.'

'Cousin. Please. Cleo will think I am always sour and serious.'

'Imagine.' Sofia rolled her eyes, her tone dry. 'Have you seen him laugh, Cleo?'

Cleo's heart squeezed. She had. They'd laughed quietly together as she lay in his arms, about some silly anecdote she'd told him about her work. Laughed as they'd showered together in her small bathroom. Laughed, standing at the window of her flat, at the antics of the seagulls, the only other creatures awake.

'Now I have,' she said with forced lightness, avoiding the tell, but her cheeks felt hot. Thankfully Isabella chose that moment to stir in the bassinet and Sofia was instantly distracted.

Felipe raised his brows at her pink cheeks and smiled at her until her cheeks heated even more. 'Stop it,' she mouthed.

But inside she warmed as well because some of the instant rapport they'd shared on Saturday night had returned since the birth on the street.

She turned her head quickly to look out the window before her red cheeks caused comment from Sofia, but there was still that full awareness of the man sitting next to her.

His thigh next to hers, though not touching. The warmth of his nearness, the powerful shifts of his body, the scent of his cologne, which she would never forget.

When the baby had settled and peace returned to the rear of the car, Felipe touched her shoulder.

She pulled her thoughts from how she could extricate herself from the mess she'd landed in and looked at him.

'Will you plan an outing tomorrow, now that Sofia will be spending time with her grandmother?'

She was struggling with this shift between them. She didn't know if she had the headspace for tomorrow right now.

'Perhaps. We will see how Isabella is through the night tonight.'

He started to say something then stopped and said, 'Of course.'

He settled back and said no more and she wondered what he had been going to say. Then stopped herself.

The next morning Sofia rose bright and happy and Isabella lay content in her carry bassinet. Cleo had risen each time Isabella had woken in the night and with subtle suggestions Sofia had grown more confident to settle the baby quickly and for longer periods between. Unfortunately, it was harder each time for Cleo to fall back to sleep. The odd way Felipe had watched her after the birth of Elena's baby kept returning to unsettle her; even his voice had changed when he'd spoken to her.

Perhaps she could leave by the end of the week as Sofia was doing so well.

After breakfast, Cleo stood at the upstairs window and watched Sofia and Isabella be driven away by Felipe's driver. Sofia had grumbled a little at it being just eight thirty and Cleo smiled at the early start Felipe's grandmother had demanded. She was clearly wasting no more time.

Was the house empty of its master? Cleo hadn't seen Felipe leave. Blue skies and sunshine tempted her to see something of the city and be back before lunch. Sofia had cleverly downloaded a taxi app to Cleo's phone so she could summon a lift when she wanted to move about the city.

Cleo liked that idea of the freedom to see what she wished and then to call a driver when she needed to move on.

A knock sounded at the door and, on opening it, Maria handed her a note. She took it reluctantly. Even though she'd never seen his writing before, she knew it was from Felipe.

So he was still at home and she would not escape from him so easily. She really shouldn't be excited by the thought of that but her darned pulse rate had jumped unmistakably.

'Tea is served in the library,' Maria said, and turned away.

Cleo unfolded the paper.

I wish to speak to you. F

She could actually hear her heart beating. Well, that was the end of a quiet sightseeing tour around Barcelona on her own. Maybe he would suggest she wasn't needed any more, which would be the most sensible thing because she was finding it harder and harder not to remember certain intimate moments between them.

She descended the stairs, took a deep breath and opened the library door.

'Good morning, Cleo.'

'Good morning, Don Felipe.'

He raised his brows at her. 'Perhaps if I kissed you every time you called me Don, you would stop doing it.'

She raised her brows back. 'I would stop because if you did that I would not be here to call you anything.'

'I believe that, too.' The smile he gave her made her tingle. 'Did you sleep well?'

'Yes, thank you,' she lied.

'Neither did I.' Matter-of-factly. He smiled broadly at her and it was the first truly open smile she'd seen since her apartment in Coogee. Despite herself, she laughed.

'I'm sorry to hear that.'

He nodded but didn't comment. 'So today, at least until Sofia returns, I would like to spend the morning with you.' There was no question in the statement and she shook her head at his arrogant assumption.

'Not "May I spend time with you?"' The way he was looking at her now made her think that sightseeing was the last thing on his agenda. His tone reminded her of the night they'd first met. The dashing dancer hero, arrogant, overpoweringly handsome, offering her wine and suggesting they take a walk. She'd gone that time, had been a fool once, and doing the same thing in Barcelona while in his employ would be doubly foolish. But she was seriously tempted to blow him a kiss and say yes.

'I have already made plans.' Her voice hadn't sounded as definite as it should have, if she was being honest with him or herself.

'Really?' His brows rose but his smile stayed. He was playing with her. 'What are they?'

Her mind raced as she tried to remember the places she wanted to see. 'I have an app on my phone for the taxis going into the city and I'm going to the Sagrada Familia.'

His face softened. 'Gaudi's most beautiful church is certainly worth a visit. May I come with you?'

'Do I have a choice?' She shook her head again at his cheek but happiness bubbled up and she gave in to it. Why should she miss out on this man's company and his no doubt stellar tourist-guide capabilities? The chance of spending time alone with Felipe made her belly tingle. She was a fool, yes. But a lucky one.

'Of course. But I would like to come with you.' And there he was, giving with one hand and taking away with the other. His handsome face laughing up at hers. Making her sigh with what could have been between them—if only. Spending the day with him would only make it harder to leave him in the end.

'Why aren't you at work?'

'I spent several hours there in the early hours of this morning and I have just returned from there again. I am going back this afternoon.'

She instantly saw the sudden flattening of his mood. Her heart sank. 'Don Raymond?'

'*Sí*. He is at rest now.'

She leaned in and touched his arm. 'I'm so sorry for your loss.'

He looked down at her. 'Thank you. He has told me many times to appreciate his presence and not moan about his departure.'

She smiled but it was very hard. She had the feeling Felipe didn't have too many true friends.

She gave in to the cause of diverting his thoughts. 'What time would you like to leave?'

He looked at his watch. 'The earlier the better. As soon as Carlos returns with the car. The crowds grow large as the day wears on.'

Huge crowds did not sound fun. 'Why is that?'

'In the Sagrada tickets allocate a time to go in but not a time to leave. One could lose a full day inside.'

She nodded. She just needed to collect her handbag. 'Then as soon as possible sounds ideal.'

'Good.' He smiled at her. 'Another day I would like to take you at sunset to see the golden light streaming in through the windows.'

Another day? Was he planning more trips? Instead of asking that, she only commented, 'You sound enamoured of the place.'

'I will tell you that story later.'

Half an hour later they were seated together in the rear of Felipe's car. He touched her hand. 'Today we relax. Not business. Just friends.'

Could she do that? Pretend this Spanish aristocrat was just a friend of hers? Cleo Wren, Australian midwife, sightseeing in Barcelona with Felipe, her sexy flamenco dancer?

This was how they'd started all this. With a dancer she'd found irresistible and a walk, holding hands.

The chemistry between them sizzled and crackled just sitting in the car. His body heat so near to her thigh, his mouth curved and wickedly teasing. His eyes watching hers with a banked desire.

What would a morning of dropping the barriers between them do to their relationship? Or was she too much of a coward to find out?

'We can try,' she said.

When they arrived, parking behind one of the huge tourist buses, Felipe was the one who hopped out swiftly and opened her door, leaving Carlos ready to pull back into the traffic. She guessed he would be picking them up later. So that meant it was just Felipe and her.

The car disappeared around the corner in the rush of traffic and Felipe took her hand and threaded her through the vehicles when the lights turned red on the corner.

He didn't let go of her fingers and the heat from that steady pressure travelled the length of her arm.

'Aren't you afraid people will see you holding my hand?'

'Tourists? No.'

'I thought you are a famous person here?' Indeed, women were already looking at him but not so much with recognition as appreciation.

He smiled at her. 'It is true I know people, and many know me, too, but you are my friend from Australia and what is the use of trappings and responsibilities of wealth if one cannot use them? Also, we have early access to a tourist site.'

He strode to the exit gate. Nodded to the guard and of course they were waved straight in. She wanted to stand outside and gawk for just a moment at the Sagrada before going inside. It was huge. Incredible.

'You come here often?'

He smiled, his eyes amused and also reminiscing about the past. 'My nurse, my nanny who looked after me when I was a child, she brought me many times because it was her Sunday church. She still prays here weekly. Before she worked for us, and afterwards, too, she told me stories of the church. There were many stories. I have a house here she resides in now.'

His face had softened again, a smile reaching to the lines playing around his eyes as he thought back to those times. 'This place gives such peace to the soul, this temple.'

Temple. She savoured his use of the word. The Sagrada was a temple. Soaring into the sky with ornate towers and the intricate sculpture that seemed to decorate every wall and surface no matter how high or wide she looked. But huge coloured fruit? On top of the towers?

'Come. We will enter from this side instead of the other where the crowds and tour guides are holding their discussions before going inside.' He drew her up the steps, pointing out the apostles and Christ and the myriad stories carved into the stone, and she saw yet another facet of Felipe. The man touched by his childhood church.

He was indeed an enthusiastic Catalonian. Like the dancer she'd first met. Proud and eager to share something he loved with someone who appreciated it. 'I will take you to the other entrance when we come back at sunset another day.'

Then they were inside, and Cleo's breath caught in her throat.

It was as if she stood in the middle of a giant cathedral forest with huge white trees holding up the golden roof of the world. The corded trunks of the enormous central columns reached up, drawing her eyes to the lace of the ceiling. Hundreds of multicoloured windows spilled light into the centre and the people were dappled in shifting leaves of colour. The morning sun painted beams across the floor and the walls and the rows of pews in blues and greens and golds and reds. Her breath caught in wonder.

Oh, my. She held her chest at the wonder of it. 'I wish I could lie on the floor and just gaze up.'

CHAPTER EIGHTEEN

FELIPE DRANK IN the expression of wonder on her face. Found just what he'd hoped he'd find. Saw the awe and the way her eyes caressed the magnificent walls and ceiling of the Sagrada. There was even a glint of tears in her sapphire eyes.

He watched her crane her head awkwardly, almost overbalancing, and moved behind her and pulled her back against his chest to steady her. 'Lean on me. Look.'

And then she was resting against him. His arms came around her and he held on lightly to her hips, her beautiful hips, his fingers feeling the heat of her curves, soaking in the firmness of bone beneath his hands. He knew these hips.

The scent of her filled his lungs until his mouth dried with his need to taste her again. Hot, explicit memories flooding him of the night neither of them had slept.

God would forgive him for having carnal thoughts in a holy place. His nanny would be horrified. How could he have been such a fool to think that he would ever be able to forget Cleo?

In his defence there had been much he'd needed to do in his rush back to Barcelona, but he was beginning to realise that even if he had flown back to Spain without her, another trip to Australia would have happened before too long. And she would not have slipped away from him because Diego and his Jen were his link to her.

'And you say your nanny used to come here on Sundays for the service?' Her soft voice, still reverent with respect for the beauty around her, broke into his thoughts. Cleo would have been scandalised with his thoughts in this place of God, too. Or maybe not. Perhaps one day he would find out.

'*Sí.* Every week. For the worship.'

'How amazing would that feel. To be a part of a service here.' She sighed and leaned back more firmly against him and the irony of her forgetting she was being held by him, oblivious to the feelings he had for her, mocked his control. Her rapt attention remained on the ceiling and the walls, and every now and then she shifted against him to change the angle of her body and he tried not to groan out loud.

His body responded despite himself, and he had to force his hands to relax against her body. 'A Sunday service? Yes, that can be arranged.' He would do that for her.

Minutes later she whispered, 'I can see why you said those that come inside stay for hours.' She moved her head in wonder and her hair brushed his face. He wanted to take one of the strands in his fingers, roll it around and then kiss it but he inhaled the scent of her instead. As she spoke her body settled more firmly against his.

'It would take days, weeks, perhaps even months of study to observe most of the intricacies inside and out.'

'Sí,' he agreed, but he could hear that his voice had grown taut with his need to turn her around and see into the depths of her eyes. To taste her mouth. Flatten her breasts against his chest.

So where could this madness lead?

An affair lasting just a few days? Weeks? Possibly months?

Or to a wonderful life for two people who loved and laughed together?

Or perhaps it might end in a nightmare of a marriage like his parents had suffered. The factor that had kept him single all these years. No. He was not his father—but he also knew that after Cleo's own painful marriage, her freedom was important to her. Her whole world was in Australia.

Could the woman in his arms live in Spain? For ever? With him? He could not live permanently in Australia with all his family responsibilities. Suddenly all the very good reasons why he shouldn't have started this liaison came crashing back.

He gently put her aside and she blinked and focussed again. Stepped another pace back as she realised she'd been held by him and had enjoyed it. Had used him mindlessly as she'd lost herself in the architecture.

As if she had felt utterly safe in his arms.

That made him smile and want to snatch her back. Foolish woman didn't even know when she was in danger.

He cleared his throat. 'In the afternoons the light streams in from the other side. It paints the walls and the floor like this does now, but in different colours.'

Her sigh was long and heartfelt. Filled with wonder. 'It's the most beautiful building I've ever seen,' she said.

'*Sí.* It is a masterpiece.'

She stepped further away from him, saw the tension in his face, but then her eyes strayed again, and he almost had himself back under control despite the 'oh' noise she breathed, and he raised his brows as her gaze came back to his.

She put her hand over her mouth as she noted what her gyrations against him had cost his self-control.

'Your fault,' he teased.

Her face went pink and he enjoyed her consternation.

'Oh. I'm so sorry. I was using you as a leaning post.' Her cheeks grew even pinker and he wanted to touch the warm skin and feel the heat.

'I enjoyed it.' He tormented her, unable to help himself, then took her hand again as they wandered amidst the soaring columns past the tourists and the guides and the security. Occasionally he nodded at someone in the crowd but his attention remained on Cleo.

After another hour he glanced at his watch. 'Is there more you wish to see here today?'

He saw her peer down at her own watch and her beautiful eyes widened. 'Oh, no, you've been very patient.'

'It is no hardship.'

Her face was soft, content, at peace. With her hand in his she said, 'It's beautiful. And I can tell you love it here, too.'

He'd loved being here with her. 'That as well. But perhaps coffee before we head back to pick up Sofia?'

CHAPTER NINETEEN

WHEN THEY CAME out again into the bright sunshine Cleo couldn't help looking back at the soaring, lacy, over-the-top façade behind her.

The Sagrada's glory stunned her with so many intricate stories woven through the architecture. Surreal in its complex vision and endless in its opportunities to find another story. And then another. And another.

Almost as surreal as allowing herself to plaster her back against Felipe's chest so she could tip her head up. As if her body had been planning the opportunity to lean into him. The solid steel of his arms keeping her balanced. The warmth of his breath against her hair. Good grief, she'd been rubbing herself against him, and he'd let her, welcomed her.

But he'd offered first and somehow she didn't think he'd disliked the opportunity.

Where was this going? Even he must see that the more time they spent together the harder it would be to forget each other afterwards.

There was no winning for either of them in any sort of long-distance relationship, living on opposite sides of the planet. She'd committed to a relationship of unequal standing before. Mark's family had badly wanted him to marry another doctor, not the midwife, and his mother had finally had her way with Mark's new wife. And that had happened in the same city, the same continent. Look where that had left her. Broken and betrayed by a trust she should never have given.

Wouldn't Felipe's important friends and his wider social set expect Don Felipe Gonzales to marry a woman of his own kind?

She couldn't take another betrayal. And this man, a man who'd picked her up and seduced her all in one night, who made the heads of every woman he passed turn and smile, and who could snap his fingers and get any woman he wanted, must be a massive risk to her heart.

What had happened to her decision to be a loner? Rely only on herself? To build a secure and fiscally sound platform that nobody could take away from her?

It would be a huge jump of faith to fall in love with and stay with a man from the other side of the world. Somebody so different culturally, socially, financially… She needed to stop whatever this was between them now.

'Thank you for taking me to the Sagrada. And for being so patient,' she said stiltedly.

He slanted a sideways glance at her, his fingers still firmly intertwined with hers.

The heat in his gaze was making her belly thrum. And his arm brushing against the side of her body was as seductive as all get out. She was having a hard time not leaning into him again. She needed distance or she'd fall against him and make him wrap his arms around her once more.

Hadn't she just had that discussion with herself?

Disaster beckoned. Cleo shook his hand to pull her own free.

He looked at her, let her go then touched her pink cheek with one finger and laughed. Pointed across the park. 'We'll go to that little restaurant there. Sit outside and you can stare at the towers while you drink your coffee.'

'I'd like that.' She would. And then she could calm down. Stop thinking too much about the uncertain future and what might not go right. Take time instead to savour what was going on just at this moment.

She'd wanted to see the sights of Barcelona and he seemed to know instinctively how to improve her experience.

She walked, her empty hand now feeling strangely bereft, and as she did so, she breathed slowly and calmly and settled her raging hormones as best she could. She was probably reading far too much into what had happened.

Perhaps he would have had the same reaction to any woman who'd leaned against him like she'd done. And yet a small voice inside whispered that she did Felipe a disservice.

When they were settled under the leafy green of an overhanging tree she sat back in her chair and gazed across the park at the Sagrada.

'It's such a crazy, wonderful, amazing building. Like the little of Barcelona that I've seen.' And felt. Just like Felipe was wonderful.

He echoed her thoughts. 'Like what is between us?' His voice floated across the tablecloth in a deep, teasing murmur.

Her gaze sprang from the building to his face. 'You think so?'

'I know so.' He pointed to it and then at the two of them. 'Crazy. Wonderful. Amazing.' He repeated the words back at her.

'It's all rather a pickle,' she said softly. Sighed heavily and shook her head as he watched her with a smile playing around his sexy lips.

Before she could think what to say next the waitress reappeared to take their order and saved her.

By the time the orders were taken Cleo wasn't sure whether it would help or create more damage by bringing up the subject of that one night that always seemed to shimmer between them, even here at a small café table in front of the Sagrada.

'So,' he said, and picked up the glass of freshly

poured water in front of him, 'in my house…' he sipped, put the glass down, then stared straight into her eyes '…do you think of me when you're in your bed?' Felipe obviously had no qualms about asking such a personal question and she could feel her poor cheeks, the same ones that had only just cooled down, heat up again. For goodness' sake!

His words lifted the hairs on her arms. She could lie. Pretend she was oblivious to his charms, but he would know that was a farce.

Instead she lifted her face to his and held his gaze. Then to pay him back she picked up her own glass, never taking her eyes off him, sipped, and said coolly, 'Why wouldn't I? You're a wonderful lover.'

He didn't smile, like she'd thought he would. She went on in a more serious tone. 'Now I work for you. So I am not the same person who slept with you that night.'

'We did not sleep.'

With that comment her anger and frustration flared. 'What exactly do you want from me, Felipe?'

The waitress arrived with their coffees and hurried off.

He leaned forward, his mouth near hers. 'And that is the best question you have asked all day.'

'Why?' She stirred her coffee briskly and almost threw down the spoon.

'Because it is my question, too, and I do not know the answer.'

She pushed away the small confectionery that had accompanied the coffee, suddenly feeling ill with the loss of something that should have been bright and shiny and filled with promise. Instead it could lead to something sordid, hiding from his grandmother and Sofia. 'There is no answer. I can't risk another night in your bed.' Because it would be an even greater wrench to leave. Even that one night they'd shared had probably spoiled her for anyone else. 'What was between us is impossible here, now and in the future.'

'And yet…' The words hung between them. 'I cannot stop thinking of how much I want you in my bed.'

Heat suffused her. 'In my experience that is not unusual for men.' She stood up abruptly. 'We should go. Your grandmother will need to rest soon and Sofia will need help with Isabella. One of us has to work.'

'I also have to work.' He threw a generous bill on the table and came around the back of her chair but she was already stepping away. Looking left and right as if the car would appear miraculously.

It did. Carlos pulled up right next to them.

Felipe opened the door for her and she scooted across, making room for him to climb in from the kerb. Who cared about those aristocratic women who blocked the door?

Once they were inside, she said, 'I believe Sofia has settled well enough for me to go home at the end of the week.'

He studied her as if trying to see what lay beneath her words. 'Why the sudden need to rush away?'

She stayed on point. Sofia. Always Sofia she should be concentrating on. 'I have nothing to add to her mothercraft skills. She is a natural.'

The car drew around the corner into a street she recognised as his grandmother's and went past the café. Except for a long streak of rubber on the road there were no signs of yesterday's accident.

They stopped in front of Doña Luisa's apartment and Carlos alighted to open Felipe's door. Felipe climbed out and then waited for her to follow.

'I'd like to stay in the car, if that's okay. Your grandmother doesn't need me to stand around while you collect Sofia and Isabella.'

He studied her and she took the opportunity to study him back. She'd ruined the morning, but he didn't seem to hold it against her. 'As you wish. Carlos will stay here.'

With the air conditioner on. She needed cooling down. Felipe walking away gave her the chance to return her breathing and her skin tone to normal. She sat in the car in solitary splendour, avoiding the eyes of the driver in front.

She stared at the plush leather and the wood trim, the cut-outs for glasses and the tiny refrigerator. The uniformed driver at Felipe's beck and call. She would be at his beck and call if she became his mistress. She was out of her league here. He was out of her league and she would not be the Australian plaything until he tired of her.

Because he would undoubtedly tire of her.

She was too far from home.

But then what was at home for her?

Felipe had suggested once that she had the right skills to work in palliative care. Where? For Felipe in the hospice? But where would she live? Could she even work in Spain? Could she shift her focus from general nursing in her medical retrieval job and occasional midwifery at the hospital to palliative care? She had already shifted in some ways with her current work.

Why not? Working side by side with Felipe. Caring for those who needed respectful acknowledgement of their own wishes and being a bridge between grieving families and the celebration of a life that was almost gone.

She stared out the window into the street, watching an older lady dressed in black snap her cane on the footpath as she walked past.

Was her Spanish good enough? This was silly. She had a flat in Coogee. Yet that was not insurmountable. She owned it or most of it anyway and could easily rent it out.

Was she being a coward and losing the chance to really see if she and Felipe had any kind of future?

Why was she so tempted to find out?

She knew why. Because she was falling in love, if she hadn't already fallen in love, with the multifaceted, incredibly wonderful Felipe Gonzales. And why was she fighting it so hard?

Because Felipe would break her if he betrayed her like the last person she trusted had.

She needed to climb onto that plane and head straight back to Australia.

Not plan how to spend more time in Felipe's company. That would surely be the end of her.

There was a tap on the window and she turned, expecting to see Felipe, but instead it was a young man who looked vaguely familiar.

'Gràcies.' The man smiled hugely at her and kept nodding. His head had a large bruise in the middle of his forehead.

Ah. Elena's husband from last night. She slipped across to the side of the car and opened the door. 'How is the mother and her baby?' she asked.

'Both well. Both well. *Gràcies.*'

'De nada.' She nodded back. 'Congratulations to Elena and to you.' The man smiled again, before moving on.

Felipe appeared beside her, glaring at the man as he hurried away almost as if he wanted to follow him and demand to know what he was doing.

'He's the husband from last night, remember? Elena and her baby are doing well.'

Felipe's brow cleared. His stiff shoulders relaxed. 'Of course.' Had he been jealous? A little thrill of pleasure ran through her. Did he care enough about her to want to warn off other men? 'I should have told you,' he said. 'I rang the hospital and checked their condition. They must live around here.' His admiring look made her feel warm. 'They won't forget you.'

'Or I them.'

But she thought again of his instant alertness towards the man who'd spoken to her. Surely he hadn't been jealous? Maybe he was just concerned for her safety. But not with Carlos there…

'Where is Sofia?'

'She has decided to stay here with my grandmother. Doña Luisa has deteriorated I think since last night. Perhaps now that the visit she was waiting for has come to pass she can finally relinquish the struggle. Sofia wants to stay with her.'

He circled the car and slipped into the back seat next to her.

So Sofia wasn't coming?

And she, Cleo, Sofia's mothercraft helper, wasn't with her.

What just happened there? she wondered as the car pulled away from the kerb.

'Shouldn't I stay and assist Sofia, if she is staying at your grandmother's?'

'The baby is asleep and my grandmother also is asleep in her chair. Sofia was holding her hand. I think she has realised that there is not much time left.'

Ah. That was it then. She wasn't needed any more. 'I should go home.'

He turned to face her fully. His eyes were dark and determined. 'I would prefer if you did not leave. You still have most of your contract to fulfil. I would be indebted to you if you could settle Sofia into my grandmother's apartment. That is what they both wish now, she tells me, but she will need your help. Especially now.'

He sighed, and now he'd erected a barrier to prevent his emotions showing, but she knew he was preparing himself for the loss of Doña Luisa, the most important woman in his life. 'It is not an easy thing for the uninitiated to understand the finality of death.'

That was true. 'Especially a new mother.'

'I agree.' He smiled slightly but the hint of sadness was back in his eyes, and she wanted to lay her hand on his arm in comfort, but his arm moved away as if he knew what she was thinking. That hurt. Which was a warning she should take heed of.

'I have a proposition for you.' His gaze held hers. 'Would you consider assisting the nurses in the care of my grandmother at the end of her life? Sofia wishes to stay, but it is too much with a new baby, and the actual nursing, she has no idea what that entails, but she wants you with her.'

Cleo frowned.

'It is not what you came here for.' This time he lifted her hand and briefly squeezed her fingers. He was still allowed to touch her, it seemed. His warmth seeped into her. 'Will you do this for our family?'

Not what she had come here for, no, yet she had come to help Sofia. And that young woman's need would be great if she wanted to stay with her grandmother until the end. 'May I have some time to think about it?'

'Of course.' He nodded.

Something in his voice alerted her to a trace of humour. 'I'm not sure I trust the way you said that. How long have I got to decide?'

He smiled at her. 'It will take half an hour for us to arrive at my house, where we are to pack Sofia and Isabella's things. That should be long enough.'

She looked at him exasperatedly. 'Really?'

'I did not arrange this but I can see, if you are willing to be taken advantage of again, how much it will help us all.'

So many reasons for not doing this. The greatest one seated beside her. And perhaps so many reasons to stay if she was brave enough. 'But your grandmother doesn't really know me.'

'She does not know the nurses either and Sofia has told her of your care during her labour.' He shrugged. 'They have cooked this up between them so be sure that my grandmother is choosing to do what she wishes. She is not a woman who pleases other people for the sake of politeness.'

She shook her head at him. 'This suits you, too, though. Doesn't it?'

The glint in his eyes had nothing to do with his grandmother. 'That you are here for an extended time? Yes.'

Was he seeing possibilities between them or did he really believe she would be of benefit to his grandmother and his family? Or both?

She probed further. 'I would be a stranger, looking after your grandmother in her final hours...'

Now he turned serious. 'You are no stranger to me. You are no stranger to Sofia.' He smiled at her and the warmth and depth of his appreciation made her breathless.

'I believe that very shortly you will not be a stranger to Doña Luisa either and she, too, will sing your praises.'

CHAPTER TWENTY

NOW THAT HE had Cleo in Spain he didn't want her to leave again. Hated the thought with a passion that surprised him and yet didn't.

Sofia's request had shocked him but the more he thought about it the more sensible he could see it was.

He loved his grandmother and he wanted her to have the comfort she deserved in her final days. His grandmother's very efficient nurse lacked the heart of the woman beside him.

That his cousin also wanted to be there for the difficult time ahead, losing her grandmother before her eyes, impressed him, and his cousin's common sense in asking for Cleo made him look at Sofia in a new light. She was growing up fast.

'I know this is a lot to ask.' He believed she would do it. He would pay her well, but already he knew that held no factor of influence in her decision.

Cleo leaned back into the chair beside him and closed her eyes for a moment. 'I'll do it. I'll stay.

And I will do everything in my power to keep your grandmother comfortable.'

He had no doubt she would. Felt relief wash over him. And not just for his grandmother. For himself, too. 'Thank you.'

'Then I will go home.'

He would worry about the last statement later.

He watched a worried frown cross her face like a small cloud and wanted to smooth the wrinkled skin.

Felipe added, 'I will contact your place of work about the change. Though they will wish to confirm it with you, of course.' He considered how much he was asking her to trust him again.

'And so that you know you can go at any time I will book an open first-class ticket for you to use whenever you wish.'

'Are you reading minds now?'

He laughed. She was a treasure. 'If I were you, I would want those questions answered.'

'Thank you.' Her turn to smile. 'While I am needed and wanted, I accept your terms.'

'Thank you.' He pulled out his phone. 'I will phone ahead and have Maria pack Sofia's luggage. Would you like me to ask her to pack yours, too?'

She shifted in her seat and he saw her discomfort. Despite his usual impatience, he paused. 'I can wait if you prefer to pack your own.'

She smiled at him and it was worth the frustration of standing around when he had so many other things to do.

'I would prefer that.'

He took out his phone and while his conversation with Maria was conducted, he studied her profile.

She chewed on the edge of her lip and he wanted to touch that gentle flesh and tell her to stop but he didn't want to stir up all her reservations again.

She wasn't the only one thinking about how much more difficult this would be when the time came for her to leave. Yet deep inside that feeling of relief continued to spread through him. Tendrils of calm that he recognised came from the presence of the woman beside him.

Perhaps because now he could share the truly heartbreaking goodbye to his grandmother with someone who understood. Strange how he was so sure this was true about a woman he had known for so short a time.

He did not know how he knew but he did. Knew in his heart it was true.

She would be with him when the time came. There was deep comfort in that thought because before Cleo there had been nobody he would have turned to for comfort.

Less than a week ago he hadn't even known that he needed anybody.

The car stopped at the bottom of his stairs and

Maria already stood at the door with the first of the luggage. He would go to his office and arrange the things he'd promised Cleo he would arrange. Hopefully, by the time he had done that she would be ready to go.

CHAPTER TWENTY-ONE

HALF AN HOUR later Cleo walked down the steps of Felipe's palatial home and wondered if she would ever see it again.

When she got to the bottom, instead of sliding straight into the car, she stopped and turned back. The footman put her small case in the boot and then disappeared around the side of the house.

Above her, the stairs reached steeply to the front door, the windows glinted above and to the right of the façade on the second floor she could see the room that had been hers with a small balcony that had looked over Barcelona.

She'd be living down amidst all those buildings and people for the next little while before she went home to Australia.

She didn't like to put a time limit on it, but she was thankful to be able to stay a little longer, thankful that she could help these people who had come into her life like brilliant comets and would no doubt shoot out again just as quickly when all this was over.

She thought about this morning with Felipe at the Sagrada, was fiercely glad she'd have that time to look back on later, but playing this game with the dancer Felipe was over.

She thought about Sofia's confident mothering but also the young woman's need to have a sounding board, seeing as she was without a partner to be that support person.

Yes, there was still some need for her there.

And she thought about Doña Luisa facing life's greatest challenge and what she could do as a silent pillar of support for others. Surprisingly she felt at peace about her choices.

None of this was about her.

So that meant none of this was about Felipe either.

It was all about Doña Luisa and Sofia creating memories that would carry the young mum through the next weeks, months and years of remembering her grandmother.

She turned back to the car. Felipe, already seated in the back, offered her a quick smile. 'Your place of work has agreed. They will email you, and your flight has also been arranged.'

'Thank you.'

'De nada.' Then he returned his attention to studying his phone. He didn't speak and she was glad of that.

She had her own thoughts to occupy her.

* * *

A short time later, when they arrived at the apartment in the city, they were met at the door by Alba, who seemed perhaps a few degrees warmer than she had been on Cleo's first visit.

'I'll see you in a few minutes.' Felipe went on ahead to see his grandmother.

Alba directed Cleo to her room. 'Señorita, Sofia and the infant are across the hall from you. Doña Luisa's room is at the end of the hallway.'

The room she was shown to seemed too large, filled with light, and had two open slatted doors as well as the tiniest balcony. A small round table and one spindly chair had been squeezed onto the balcony overlooking the street.

Carlos deposited her cabin bag at the door and carried the rest into Sofia's room.

Alba opened a connecting door to a generous private bathroom tiled in green and gold, with a sink with gold taps similar to the one she had washed in after Elena's baby's birth.

'Thank you, Alba. How is Doña Luisa?'

Alba scowled. 'She is resting. The nurse has left her exhausted from washing her. I would do better than that lump.'

Goodness. Not a reassuring reference from Alba. 'And Miss Sofia?'

'In the library, talking to the woman.'

'Thank you.'

Alba nodded and left. Cleo considered if there

would be more help for Alba in running the house if two more guests were added to her workload. Cleo could lift some of that load, too, if she was allowed to. But first she wanted to talk to Sofia and the nurse.

She quickly unpacked, hung her few things in the wardrobe and slid her small toiletries case into the bathroom, then tied back her hair and washed her hands. It was time to see what she could do to help. If possible, she'd like to slide discreetly into the household without alienating anyone. They'd had disruptions enough.

She could hear the nurse before she saw her. Her voice held an aggrieved tone as she gesticulated to Sofia and waved in the direction of the kitchen.

When Cleo arrived, the nurse, a tall, uniformed, big-boned thirty-something Spaniard with dark hair and an unsmiling mouth, did not appear pleased to see her.

Cleo tried not to feel depressed at her unwelcoming stare.

Cleo smiled and held out her hand. '*Bon dia.* Do you speak English?'

'Yes.'

'Hello, then, I'm Cleo.' She held out her hand and reluctantly the woman took it. 'I was Sofia's midwife and am now her guest. You are Doña Luisa's nurse?'

The woman nodded curtly. 'I am Rhona. They say you are to help me?'

'Lovely to meet you, Rhona. I understand Doña Luisa is not well today?'

'She is failing. There was much excitement yesterday. Today she is happy to sleep.' A hard stare. 'Don Felipe tells me you are to help.'

'I am here to support Sofia, who wishes to help. Between the three of us I'm sure we can make Doña Luisa comfortable and feel cared for, without exhausting Sofia, as a new mother, as well. Don't you agree?'

'Oh, yes. I see.' A lot of the starch left Rhona at that. Gently, Cleo asked, 'I'm sure you have much experience nursing terminal patients at home?'

'Not in the home, no, but in the aged care hospital.'

Cleo smiled. 'Aged care is a special field. You must be very caring.'

Rhona unbent another fraction. 'It is important to remember that one day this will be yourself at the mercy of the nurse. And act accordingly.'

'I couldn't agree more. I am a midwife and nurse, so I understand when someone we are caring for is vulnerable and needs reassurance and the support of others.

'Would you agree, Sofia?'

'I know it helped me to have you there.' She nodded. 'Even though you couldn't take the pain or do the work of labour, I never felt afraid. This is what I hope to share with my grandmother.'

The last of Rhona's stiffness left her. '*Sí*. This is what I wish, too.' She sighed and looked at Cleo. 'I accept your help and the support of Nurse Sofia as we all care for Doña Luisa.'

Then, almost shyly, 'It is true I found her weakness made the work much heavier this morning. Perhaps it would be more gentle on her to have assistance when she cannot help herself.'

'And I will be a support for Sofia as she sees for the first time the transition from life to death.'

The nurse stared at her as she thought about that.

'Yes. That, too, is a good thing.' She dipped her head. 'I'm sorry I was not more welcoming.'

'You have nothing to apologise for. Thank you for your understanding of my presence.'

Felipe entered the room at that moment and Cleo searched his face for signs of distress or concern. He looked tired but not cast down. As an oncologist he would see this often. But as a grandson this was a first, and a tragedy. 'She wishes to see you, Cleo.'

Cleo glanced at Rhona and the woman waved her in.

'I will eat and drink tea and then perhaps we can make her more comfortable when next we reposition her.'

Felipe escorted Cleo back along the magnificent hallway past paintings and priceless objects to the darkened room. He paused outside the door. 'I have no idea how you did it but I do believe Rhona likes you. The nurse certainly seems more than resigned to your arrival now.'

'We are all here for the same reason. To care for your grandmother to the best of our ability.'

He smiled. 'Still, you have done well to smooth feathers that my grandmother said were very ruffled.' He gestured with his head towards the door and lowered his voice even further. 'There has been a rapid decline but perhaps it is as the nurse says and she is simply exhausted from all the excitement yesterday.'

He smiled in reminiscence. 'She was very excited to meet the baby and have Sofia back in Spain. You have helped there, too.'

'I'm glad. Are you coming in with me?'

'No. Go alone. I will wait out here.'

The darkened room of Doña Luisa held the scent of lavender and the aroma of candle smoke. The smoke came from a small altar with two candles and a gilt-framed image of Jesus.

Cleo hadn't thought about the Catholic significance of terminal illness in Spain but she should have. She could see how that would be a large part of Doña Luisa's transition out of this world.

As a non-Catholic she'd have to ask Felipe or the nurse later if there was anything she needed to be aware of regarding Doña Luisa's religious needs. Perhaps the emergency number of her priest as well.

She passed further into the room and saw the papery skin and yellow tinge of Doña Luisa's skin against the pillow. Her breath caught and she eased it out discreetly. The physical change from a woman who'd walked with a stick to one lying in a bed barely able to raise herself up on her elbows was stark.

'Come closer, so I can see you.' Doña Luisa's feeble voice called her towards the bed.

There was an ornate but strategically placed chair so Cleo sat, creating enough space not to crowd Doña Luisa but close enough for easy conversation.

A swathe of silver hair lay tucked into one side of her pale face. Lines of tiredness—she didn't think they were of pain—were etched deeper into her cheeks.

'Good afternoon, Doña Luisa. Is there anything special you would like me to do?'

The older woman huffed out a small laugh. 'You seem to be achieving what needs to be done. There is nothing wrong with my hearing and my grandson thinks you've calmed the nurse.'

On that tart note she closed her eyes. With eyes still shut, she said, 'I am glad you are here to help my family. To help Sofia, but most of all to help my grandson. When I am gone, he will have no one he allows close.'

Cleo didn't know what to say to that. She didn't think he allowed her close either.

'He watches you constantly. Do not discount the power you have to help him.' Then she sighed.

'My wash tired me. Rhona means well but she pulls me around like a sack. You will help her be more gentle.' Another sigh. 'I will sleep and talk with you later. The pain medication makes me drowsy.'

'Do you have pain at the moment?'

'No. It has left for the time being.'

'Good.' Cleo assessed the sheets pulled up to the pale chin and noted the freshness and precision of the tucking in. Signs of an old-school nurse.

Though Doña Luisa's tidily brushed hair and the lingering soapy smell of lavender attested to the thoroughness of the sponge bath, a little looseness in the sheets and perhaps a chink of gentle light would be good. She'd suggest that diplomatically later. For the moment there was nothing she could do except let her sleep.

Seeing Felipe's grandmother surrounded by the things she loved, comfortable and fresh, with her family in attendance was comforting to everyone as well as for Doña Luisa. It must be helpful to know all the resources she needed were here and there was no reason to move to a hospital for the end unless she wanted to.

Cleo rose. 'Rest well.' But the woman in the bed was already asleep.

Sofia and Felipe waited for her outside the door. The young mum was leaning on the wall while absently patting her baby's bottom. She straightened when Cleo came from the room. 'How is she?'

'Tired. She's sleeping.'

'How could she have gone so quickly downhill?' Sofia asked.

'Sometimes it is the way,' Felipe said quietly.

'And she tells me there is nothing wrong with her hearing so I shall move away from her door.' Cleo drew them with her and smiled. 'Your grandmother is still seeing humour in the world. I hope I have the chance to know her more fully before she chooses to leave us.'

'As I do,' he said as they all moved to the main rooms. Felipe glanced at his watch. 'I must go.'

And that was that. It shouldn't have shocked her, but it did. Had she become so used to him being around?

Of course he had to go.

'I will be back tonight around seven to see my grandmother.'

This wasn't his house and he had a life. Hers was here for the next week or two. Then she would go home.

CHAPTER TWENTY-TWO

ALL AFTERNOON AT the hospice Felipe's thoughts returned to his grandmother's apartment in the city centre. Concerned for his grandmother, for Sofia and also for Cleo.

Had he been fair to Cleo to ask her to remain? Had he asked too much of a woman he had known for so little time? Yet he felt he knew her better than others he had known for years. Felt he could see to the heart of her and knew with certainty she would care for his family at this time.

And into the future, but that was for later.

He did not doubt that if anyone could ensure his grandmother's comfort and the tranquillity of the carers around her it would be Cleo. He was using her, but she didn't seem to mind. Because she gave freely to others, that was her way, as she had given herself to him, and he was learning that one day soon he would give himself to her.

Even his cousin Sofia had surprised him. She

held depths he'd not only underestimated but had failed to appreciate before.

Perhaps he was more like his father than he'd thought. Looking at members of his family as problems that needed to be solved instead of as people who needed to be considered and listened to for their wishes.

He had friends, of course, but none now who were close except perhaps Diego, but he had left Spain years ago. He had colleagues at his hospice, people who admired his work, but apart from Raymond, a man he'd shared medical school with, he had allowed very few people to get close to him. He had many acquaintances but no confidants.

Except he'd told the midwife things that he'd told no one else. That very first night in Australia.

Why was that?

Perhaps because at first he'd known he'd never see her again and some magic about her had encouraged openness. It had felt surprisingly good to be so candid with someone for once. Such was her charm. But he'd quieted his reluctance to share by saying he would leave and never see her again.

And how had that worked for him?

He almost laughed out loud. Who would have believed that a woman he'd met in an unguarded moment would change his views on life so much and become such an integral part of his life, and his family's lives, in so short a time?

And his grandmother fully approved of her. The last thing he had expected from a woman who had been parading aristocratic Catalonian women in front of him for years.

Enough of these deep thoughts.

He was better here, working while his *àvia* slept for a few hours. Waiting for a phone call in case his grandmother's condition changed, seeing to other patients' needs and grieving families, daily staff and administrative issues that had piled up in his absence, Felipe worked steadily to free himself from the overload, and in between short conversations with Alba to check he prayed for his grandmother.

When he returned to his grandmother's apartment just before five that evening the lift doors opened to the faint strains of 'Nights in the Gardens of Spain' by Manuel De Falla. The recording had been one of his grandmother's favourites but he hadn't heard it played in her apartment for years.

The volume was turned so low it was almost a murmur but the whispering orchestra added an undercurrent of life and soul into the darkness of the approaching night.

Alba's mouth twitched when she saw he recognised the music, though her eyes were sad. 'The priest has been. And now the baby has been lying next to her,' she said.

Felipe followed her silently to the door of the darkened bedroom, where he leaned against the frame. He could hear his grandmother's laboured breathing but the scene was peaceful.

Alba slipped away, no doubt to the kitchen.

In the corner the nurse sat knitting and back from the bed. Cleo reposed calmly, with hands crossed, almost unobtrusive in the gloom, reading a small book.

In the background the subtle whisper of the music flowed over them all.

On her bed his grandmother lay on her side, packed with pillows for comfort, her face soft and relaxed, and beside her lay Isabella, one small arm free from her blanket, a tiny starfish hand clasped around her great-grandmother's finger.

The baby's eyes were wide open, and next to her on the pillows on the other side of the bed, Sofia lay asleep.

The room resonated with a gentle flow of breathing from the players in the tableau and Felipe felt serenity seep into him even though he stood on the fringes.

As if she sensed him, Cleo turned her head to meet his eyes. She smiled and the cares of the day blew from his shoulders like leaves in the wind.

He nodded his appreciation of the ambiance of the room and moved to leave them to it.

Silently Cleo stood and gestured for him to take her seat.

He waved her away but she shook her head and walked towards him, her eyes on his face. She touched his arm as she passed. 'Please, sit,' she said quietly. 'Savour the moments you deserve to share more than anyone, for they are beautiful.'

Then she walked from the room and his grandmother woke and turned her head slightly to see him. Her smile was a gift he'd almost missed.

He went closer and leaned over, kissed her cool cheek. 'Good evening, my little grandmother,' he said softly.

'It is,' his grandmother whispered as she closed her eyes and smiled. He thought she'd gone to sleep, but without opening her eyes she said, 'Thank you for bringing them to me. All of them. They are blessings.'

Her breathing became heavier but the smile remained and she soon dropped into a deeper sleep again.

He sat with her for another half an hour until the baby had fallen asleep, too, the quiet clacking of the nurse's knitting needles rhythmically soothing, not something he would have thought possible in connection with Rhona.

Cleo came to the doorway and patted her stomach, pointed to him enquiringly.

Yes, he could eat. Perhaps like a horse, because he hadn't stopped for anything since midday, and now his appetite had returned with a vengeance. He glanced at the nurse, who nodded that she would stay, and followed this amazing woman he had found across the world through to the dining room. His gaze was drawn from watching the way Cleo walked to his grandmother's empty chair.

He knew his *àvia* would not be sitting there regally to chastise him ever again.

CHAPTER TWENTY-THREE

CLEO WAITED AT the door for him to join her and when he glanced at the empty winged chair in the formal lounge she knew the direction of his thoughts. Her heart ached for him.

'Your grandmother says she feels less strong tonight,' she said. 'But there have been many moments today when we enjoyed listening to her reminiscences.' She smiled at him. 'She is a wonderful woman.'

'She is.'

'I hope you know that many of her memories centre around you. You've given her great joy.'

He inclined his head and waited for her to sit. She did but glanced up at him as he moved to his own chair. He looked so solemn and she remembered his grandmother's wish, uttered so frequently, that he should not be cast down.

She thought of the small poetry book his grandmother had asked Alba to find and give to her. She wondered if she should tell him about it.

The pages held children's poems and Doña

Luisa had said maybe one day she would read them to her own children and remember her. It was a battered book, and hadn't looked valuable, so she had accepted it in the spirit with which it was offered and thanked her. Before she could mention it, Alba carried the dishes in and set them on the table.

'Just the two of us?' He looked questioningly at the empty places.

She nodded. 'The nurse has already had her meal and Alba has put away something for Sofia when she wakes.'

'Of course, you are aware of all that goes on. You astound me.' He studied her, his eyes warm, the way they seemed to be all the time when he looked at her now. When had that changed? she wondered. Perhaps since the baby was born in the street?

He said, 'Are you a chameleon that fits into any background? You've only been here two days.'

'Everyone has been very kind.' She shook her head. 'You've missed all the fun. We have been told many secrets by your grandmother. I think Sofia will never be overawed by you again, especially after hearing of your exploits as a child.'

His smile was half-hearted. 'None of it is true.'

'Sorry.' She shook her head. 'But I believe your grandmother.'

He raised his hand ruefully and she saw a little lightening of his seriousness. 'I don't want to know what she told you. No doubt Sofia will share inappropriately later.'

Then his face changed. 'I take that back.' He frowned at himself. 'I believe I haven't appreciated Sofia enough. That will alter when I know my cousin more in the future.'

'I'm glad,' Cleo said simply. 'She's amazing. So good with the baby. So good with your grandmother.' She waggled her brows. 'And you were very good to have saved her from that man.'

He even smiled at that. 'Not what Sofia said at the time.' Then he sighed. Solemn again. 'I should have been aware of her danger earlier but that is for another time...' He turned to her and shook his head. 'I can't believe the difference I saw, walking in here tonight. Thank you, Cleo.'

Cleo felt the sting of tears and fought hard to keep them from overflowing, which they could so easily do. The last few hours had come at a cost and she was weary, but the night could prove a long one yet.

She'd be surprised if Doña Luisa saw the sun rise tomorrow.

Her greatest concern now was for this man. He loved his grandmother dearly. She'd come to realise that. She could see his needs but was trying desperately not to heighten her own feelings for someone she might still have to leave.

When she didn't answer he said, 'What you've

achieved here is a priceless gift that I can never repay.'

Her brow furrowed. 'You say that as if this organising of me being here for your grandmother is not your right.' She looked away and then thought of all the people this man helped. The insights from meeting his staff. Their love for him. The stories from his grandmother of his kindness to her. She understood him better now. Some things she'd seen for herself, some things she'd been told by others, and some things she just knew in her heart were true.

Couldn't he see? Or was he too used to keeping most people at arm's length? She remembered their first night together. Was it because his father had told him at seven not to hinder the family with his emotions as if he didn't deserve to be loved?

'You're a man who has dedicated your adulthood to creating support and quietude at the end of people's lives. If I can go some small way to providing that serenity for you here, then it is only what you deserve, and what your grandmother deserves.' She felt that with every fibre of her being. 'It is a privilege to be able to help your family. It's not a favour, Felipe.'

He looked a little stunned. 'I…' He stopped, but in the end he nodded his head and said simply, 'Thank you.'

She continued, 'I will relieve the nurse soon.

Sofia has sat with your grandmother most of today. I rested before you came home. I'll do the night shift and watch her overnight.'

'There is no need. I will stay with her.'

'Of course.' She smiled at him. Exactly what his grandmother had said he would say. 'But either the nurse or I would like to be there as an assistant if needed. It is your grandmother who requested that you have support.'

He pushed his plate away. 'I don't need support.'

'I have no doubt. I'm also hoping that you will allow me to unobtrusively follow her wishes. If that is acceptable to you.'

He looked at her from under dark brows. 'Don't use your cajoling ways on me.'

She opened her eyes wide. 'I wouldn't dream of that, Don Felipe.' She remembered too late that he'd said he would kiss her every time she called him that.

He raised his brows at her, another brief flash of humour, but then it faded.

She added, 'I'll be dozing in the corner and no nuisance to you.'

'And if I refuse to be babysat?'

She smiled. 'Then I will leave your grandmother to explain her wishes—which I'm sure she will when she wakes and finds you there alone.'

* * *

Which was how it came about that in the early hours before dawn, in that time of transition between worlds when Doña Luisa's breathing changed, that Cleo was there with Felipe. Briefly Cleo slipped away from the room.

'Sofia,' she said. The young woman looked up with startled eyes from where she was feeding her daughter and then she stilled.

'It is time?'

'Almost, I think. Would you like to take Isabella and kiss your grandmother's cheek in farewell?'

Sofia nodded and, carrying Isabella, she went in and said her last farewells beside Felipe, who sat very still in the dark.

Then Sofia touched his shoulder and left the room, tears streaming down her face. She leaned against the wall outside the door so she could sob quietly, out of her grandmother's hearing.

This brought Alba, whom Cleo had also woken at the woman's request.

Then, as per his grandmother's instructions, she stood beside Felipe as he held his grandmother's hand.

She knew she hadn't come uninvited because one unintentionally imploring glance he'd cast over his shoulder when she'd returned said how much he appreciated her support.

This was the woman who had raised him,

loved him when his father wouldn't, had been his mentor and his mother, and he was losing her.

The gap between each indrawn struggling breath grew greater, and the rise of her thin chest grew less, and then the cycle began again. They both knew the outcome and waited patiently. Felipe sat bowed with his hand in his grandmother's and Cleo stood behind him, her hand on his shoulder, until finally Doña Luisa Gonzales breathed her last.

'She has gone,' he whispered, and dropped his head to kiss the still hand beneath his.

'She will always be with you. Love is like that.'

Cleo and Sofia didn't move back to Felipe's house the next morning, though the funeral was set for four days later. Against her better judgement Cleo had agreed to stay until then.

Sofia spoke to Felipe about interviewing staff to open her house again while Cleo was there to help but he offered his cousin full access to Doña Luisa's apartment if she wished to live in the city. Sofia had been stunned but gratefully accepted the generous offer.

This way, Alba, who was lost and uncertain and grieving for her mistress, would have a new focus, to help care for Sofia and Isabella's daily needs for as long as she wished.

Cleo had seen little of Felipe, who had disappeared into Doña Luisa's office with the solicitor the first day and later with the priest to make the arrangements for the funeral. He'd then gone home to his own house after a brief goodbye.

She told herself that the distance he created between them was what she'd expected to happen. He had no need for her now. Like her husband had had no need for her when he'd found a richer, shinier woman.

But it was too late. She loved him. Had been in love with him since that first night they had lain together in her bed in Coogee, despite her denials.

He'd captured her heart by his absolute wonder in her. Their connection, though she'd tried to pretend it had just been sex, had pierced her in a way she doubted any man would be able to do again.

She wished she hadn't agreed to stay for the funeral, damn it, but Sofia had begged her not to leave yet.

They didn't see him at all the next day, though he rang and spoke to Alba and a note had come in Felipe's bold writing inviting her to lunch on the day prior to the funeral.

She'd assumed that Sofia and Isabella would be joining them.

On the day before she left Barcelona, the day she was to lunch with Felipe, Cleo woke to a brilliant blue Catalonian sky and shafts of golden light that reflected off the many mirrors and onto the ornate ceiling.

In two days she would be home at her Coogee flat, where her life would be a far cry from the elaborate halls of this city apartment or the grandeur and soaring ceilings of Felipe's mansion on the hill.

At the breakfast table a huge, barely open, long-stemmed rosebud sat to the side of both her and Sofia's plates. 'And what is this?' she asked Alba when the maid came back in with the coffee.

Alba, too, was wearing a small red rose in her buttonhole.

'April the twenty-third in Barcelona is Lovers' Day.' Alba smiled. 'Everyone gives roses. Traditionally it was the man giving a rose to his true love, and her giving him a book. Nowadays everybody gives roses, not only to lovers but to family and colleagues… It's a beautiful day!'

'Like Valentine's Day?'

'Perhaps. If you go into the city, all the stalls in the city centre will be selling roses. Sofia and I are going for a walk this morning with Isabella in the pram to see them.'

'I thought Sofia was coming to lunch with Don Felipe and me?'

'Not today,' she said, and unsuccessfully hid her smile. 'He will come at twelve and you must wait here for him.' The look she gave Cleo said clearly that she was not to go down on the street where she could get into any mischief, such as finding babies to be born.

They'd be alone?

In a town full of rose stalls?

With lovers everywhere?

Could it get any worse, with an ache in her heart that she would have to hide and her wanting more? Dreading his friendly dismissal of what had grown between them?

She had thought they had grown closer recently. Much closer. But it seemed that had been wishful thinking on her part. Apart from the note, he'd not even spoken to her since his grandmother's passing.

Once Cleo's duties were done. Her assistance given. His needs met.

But it was too late for her. She'd let her guard down, had foolishly begun to think maybe Felipe wanted more, wanted her in his life. She'd even dreamed, tentatively, of the future, but that had been before he'd distanced himself from her.

He had no need of her now.

He didn't care for her like she cared for him.

Felipe had never promised her a future.

Perhaps when she returned home it would pass. Love at first sight was impossible. Wasn't it?

Why was everything so tragic? She needed

to go home and she couldn't. Not until after the funeral.

Perhaps she should just accept the last time she would be with Felipe alone…she laughed bitterly at that…with a chauffeur, and savour her small slice of time with him to keep for ever. As long as she expected nothing.

The way he had stayed away the last couple of days had made it clear she'd done her job and she could go now. So much for a connection.

But deep inside a tiny flicker of forlorn hope refused to be extinguished. He had held her hand at the Sagrada. He had smiled at her with warmth and appreciation and wanted to see her happy. Today was their last chance. Tomorrow would be a formal occasion and then she would be gone.

She would know when he arrived.

Would he be her warm Felipe or would he be the grim-visaged aristocrat with the solid walls of formality around him?

Despite Cleo's preference to wait for Felipe downstairs, at twelve she sat in the formal lounge in her white dress, which Alba had restored to its former pristine state…and breathed.

Breathing was good. Mindful. Calming.

'A penny for your thoughts.'

She jumped. 'I must have been daydreaming. I didn't hear the lift.'

He inclined his head. 'You look lovely.'

'You look very elegant yourself.' He always

did. No matter that he wasn't formally dressed, anyone could tell he was an aristocrat. 'Where are we going?'

'We will drive around the city to show you the sights as we have kept you too busy.' So the Felipe she got was the noble showing the visitor his city. His Barcelona. His tone was formal. Not like the Felipe in Australia or the Felipe at the Sagrada. Austere.

He had said she looked lovely. But her tiny fledgling hopes of softness, of closeness between them died. 'You haven't kept me too busy.'

Sightseeing with him acting like this wasn't attractive anyway. 'Though thank you.' She allowed herself to be ushered into the lift, but she already felt like a burden to him, merely a task he felt he needed to complete.

She wished she could just get on the plane today.

He stood beside her, so tall and handsome, and she was having trouble not touching his arm, just one touch, but he was incredibly formal. Aloof. The aristocrat he was through and through, and she realised with despair that she was so not the woman for him. She should have known that. She had known that.

His reserve dashed her mood and made her want to turn back. The faint drift of his cologne teased and she wished she'd dabbed herself liberally with her own scent to drown his out. She should never have come.

He handed her into the car, past Carlos at the door, and sat back. At least Carlos seemed friendlier.

On the seat in front of her, where Sofia had sat so many times, was a huge bouquet of long-stemmed, glorious red roses.

He sat next to her. 'They are for you.'

'Lovely,' she said, trying to smile. 'But we are not lovers.' Oh, Lord, why had she said that?

CHAPTER TWENTY-FOUR

FELIPE OPENED HIS eyes wide at her flat voice. 'The roses, it is a tradition.' She didn't like roses? She'd seemed to like the ones growing at his house. 'They can also be between colleagues, even friends, and I hope I may have at least grown towards that standing with you?' Felipe was at a total loss. He'd expected her to display pleasure. Given him one of her beautiful smiles. Perhaps a kiss, or maybe that would have been too much to hope for.

He could read nothing on her face. But her mood was odd. Funny how he had trouble sensing the moods of others but with Cleo he could tell straight away when something wasn't right. He knew his nervousness to make this right today made him seem less approachable, almost grim, but he couldn't help that. He was damnably tense. On edge to do this in a way she would remember. So much depended on her answers.

'They're beautiful,' she said. But there was a lack of enthusiasm in her tone he didn't normally associate with Cleo. Was he wrong? Did she not care for him at all?

This armful of roses had been a romantic gesture prior to walking her in Gaudi's beautiful Park Güell and asking her to stay in Spain.

To ask her to allow him to take the time to court her properly. To discuss the obstacles and how they would surmount them together.

To propose marriage to her so soon after his grandmother's passing was too fast even for him—but he had come today to at least begin.

The wall between them had never been as formidable as it was now. Or was that because he so desperately wanted to break it down?

Or, more damning, was it that now she actually had her ticket home she was already gone in her thoughts? 'Is something wrong, Cleo?'

This outing was so important and yet it seemed doomed already. Already the distance between them grew wider.

'I'm tired.' She did look weary and he cursed himself for not checking on her over the last two days. 'It's been a very emotional week.' She finally looked at him. 'You must be too exhausted to play tour guide.'

That stung a little. 'I am not playing.' Nothing frivolous now, that was for sure. Though he had planned a few lighter moments that he'd thought she would appreciate.

'Like you weren't playing at being a flamenco dancer?'

He frowned at her. 'I was not playing then either. In my soul lives such a man. I thought you knew that.'

Silence. He tried a new tack. 'But that is not what I wanted to talk to you about.' Something had gone very wrong at the outset and his plans were failing fast.

'What do you want to talk to me about, Felipe?' Her tone wasn't encouraging and he wished he could take her back to the house and start again with this day. He'd thought to take her for a walk in the Park Güell with a picnic basket, and share their first kiss since far too long ago. But already he knew his plans were ashes at his feet.

'Perhaps you would consider moving to Spain and working with me at the hospice?' he said, far too abruptly. That had been one of the strategies he'd thought might interest her if she decided to stay. Stated alone, without context, it seemed overly demanding and even he had heard the harshness in his tone.

She froze. 'In what capacity?'

'I once said I could imagine you at the Hospice Luisa.' He softened his tone. Tried to make her see his vision for the future—but only if it was her vision, too. He tilted his head to study her. 'I said I could see you as one who stands at the gate and comforts those going and those who must say goodbye.'

Like she had just done so admirably for his sweet *àvia*.

She shook her head. 'No. I can't.'

'But what if you were a teacher of the gate-keepers? The mentor? Someone who shared those skills that I saw so eloquently in my grandmother's household?'

'No.' Vehemently.

He found himself pulling back from her strong denial. The word sounded like a death knell to all his hopes.

She turned away. 'This is what you wanted to talk to me about?'

'One of the things. That and perhaps moving in with Sofia.' The last thing he'd thought of when he'd realised that asking her to stay with him in his house as he courted her was not fair to either of them. But really he was floundering against her reserve.

He was very afraid now that if he mentioned love to her she would open the door and get out of the moving car.

How could he have got it so badly wrong?

Surely she wasn't immune to him? That day at the Sagrada. Her warmth and compassion in the early hours of the morning his grandmother had passed. Their one incredible night together in Sydney had affected her, he already knew that. She'd told him so on his jet.

Every day since he'd let her in a little more, accepted his need of her, his love for her, until she took up space in his world and was embedded firmly in his heart.

But perhaps he had got it wrong. Perhaps his grandmother, too, had got it wrong—though that would be a first.

Or, more likely, he felt a little of the tension in himself ease at the thought, he had simply rushed his midwife and spoiled everything.

All was not yet lost. It was just today that was lost.

That he could believe. All he could do was retreat and regroup and approach her again later. But he would not give up. If he had to follow her to Australia, then he would. He would never believe she was immune to him.

But if she left, and he followed, and she said no, then he would have to believe she did not have emotions towards him. Emotions he had seen with his own eyes—and that he shared for her.

'Have I been thoughtless in proposing we meet up today? While you are probably still tired?' He resisted the urge to grip his hair and pull it in frustration. Could he do nothing right with this woman? 'But I knew tomorrow at the funeral it would be impossible for us to talk before you left.' She didn't comment and he accepted his mistake. There is no hurry, he told himself. Give her time.

'Would you like me to take you back to the house?'

'Yes, please.'

CHAPTER TWENTY-FIVE

CLEO'S LAST DAY in Barcelona dawned dismal and dreary, like the face she saw in the mirror.

Outside, later, the sky hung leaden like her mood and the wind had a cool bite as she waited for the second black car that would carry her, Sofia and Isabella to the funeral.

A taxi would take her to the airport straight afterwards.

Her small bag was packed beside her and the tickets printed for the journey home. Tickets found also on her phone, because she liked to have the paper copies as well for extra insurance.

She'd more than fulfilled her commitments to all of the Gonzales family and she wanted to leave as soon as possible.

Even Doña Luisa's insistence that she be there for Felipe had been completed. She'd done so well there that, well, he'd offered her a job in his hospice.

Gee, thanks.

Stupid her, wishing for more. She'd known a

long-term relationship with Felipe had been a dream, but one look at the distant man who'd come to take her to lunch yesterday and she'd known he'd been lost to her.

He'd looked almost afraid she was expecting more from him than he wanted to give.

She'd been afraid he'd offer her a monetary bonus for loving them all. That would have hurt as well.

On the drive back he'd barely spoken to her, though he had caught her arm as she'd gone to get out at the apartment. 'Please, take the roses. I want you to have them.'

She'd taken them, to make him feel better. Even though they'd made her feel worse. Had buried her face in the red velvet petals in the lift as her tears had dripped onto the mosaic floor. Thank goodness nobody had been home.

He'd promised her nothing and she had no right to be disappointed that this was how it ended.

Oh. Yes. Except for the opportunity to work at the hospice and remain as a companion to Sofia.

The funeral was held in the cathedral in the centre of Barcelona and the huge church was almost full. The rows of dignitaries and heads of state felt overwhelming to Cleo. Felipe and Sofia sat in the first pew and slotted in perfectly with all the exalted personages.

Cleo fitted perfectly at the back with Alba and Rhona and Carlos.

But when the long, traditional service was done with much pomp and ceremony it wasn't over yet. Sofia had asked Cleo to go to the graveyard with her and reluctantly she'd agreed.

She could leave for the airport from the cemetery but she could not go to the wake. Enough.

Fewer people were present at the graveside service as only a few were invited to the private ceremony.

What she couldn't help notice was that apart from Sofia there was no one who approached Felipe in a genuine way to offer their condolences. Yes, there was respect, and acknowledgement of his loss, but no warmth. He really had no one. Where was the warmth?

After the greetings and handshakes he stood back from others, emitting a solitary demeanour that demanded he be left alone. Without support. Her heart ached for him but that was nothing new.

As the service closed and the first clods of earth were scattered, Sofia, with Isabella in her arms, walked up to him and touched his shoulder. Then she hugged him and, to Cleo's surprise, he hugged her back. The first time she'd seen that from him. But his face remained a forbidding mask.

Sofia kissed his cheek, said something quietly,

and then she turned and walked away to talk to other people.

Felipe remained at the graveside alone and finally Cleo couldn't stand it.

She crossed the grass, past exquisitely dressed groups of two and three people in designer black, until she stepped in front of him.

She lifted her chin and met his eyes. 'I'm so sorry for your loss, Felipe. I consider myself fortunate to have spent some time with your grandmother. She was a very strong woman.'

For the first time all day an expression crossed his face as he looked at her and the desolation in his eyes made her gasp. Unconsciously her arm rose to grip his arm and she squeezed it to comfort him with her fingers.

'Another woman I love leaves me,' he said. The wind tossed his dark hair and she shivered at his pain.

'Like you will leave me.' He'd said it very quietly and she looked up.

Startled.

'It will be a little different when I leave,' she said, 'because you don't love me.'

Instead of answering, he looked down at the grave and said, 'Now, Àvia? You think this is a good time?' Then his face softened and he whispered, 'Then rest well, my little grandmother.' He took Cleo's arm and steered her away from the crowd.

'Do you know what she said?' He didn't look at her as they walked. 'She said, "Do not let her get away."'

'Who?' Cleo was a little worried about the way this conversation was going. At the crowd they were leaving behind. Had Felipe lost it in his grief?

He looked down at her but at least his face was no longer impassive. 'No. I'm not going mad. My little grandmother told me she would haunt me if I let you get away. And I nearly did.'

She tried to pull her arm away. 'Um… I'm leaving, Felipe. My flight goes in four hours.'

'I promise that if you still wish to catch it when I am finished, I will get you there in time.'

He ushered her with his hand at her elbow to the car where Carlos was waiting. Felipe spoke quietly and Carlos nodded. When they were in the back seat together, Carlos shut the door and stood a few paces in front of the car door to prevent anyone approaching them.

He turned to her, then took both her hands in his. She lifted her chin. 'What?'

'You are never afraid, my midwife. And I would never do anything to make you afraid.' He kept hold of her hands but more gently now. 'I see I must work harder for you. Must open myself up, but I find this so hard.' His eyes searched hers.

'I don't understand.' She didn't.

'Yesterday, inside I was a young lover playing

Romeo, yet on the outside I came across as cold and forbidding as my father.'

'Romeo?' She shook her head. 'Where was he during that conversation?' A small glimmer of light hit her.

He smiled. 'Emotion of the heart. It is hard for me to show. It makes me sound formal when I try to let it all out.' He shrugged without releasing her fingers.

'You were nothing like Romeo yesterday.'

Then he smiled and his face finally opened up to show the man she loved. 'But I will work on it. You will help me. You will always bring out the passionate dancer in my soul. If anyone can do it, it is you. For you are my angel. My midwife.'

She shook her head. Too much. Too fast. Too dangerous to believe in.

'You see my problem?'

She still felt confused.

'I love you.' He shrugged those beautiful shoulders and she felt her pulse speed up.

Three crazy words she'd never expected him to say. But he didn't give her time to question him.

'I did not know, until after that babe was born in the street, that I love you with all my heart. I have done ever since that first night.'

Nope. He'd left her without even a word. 'I don't believe you.'

'Did you know, that first morning, I stopped

and looked back at your window, where I had left you, and was so torn?'

How could that be true? Not one word of the future had he spoken. She would have welcomed even one.

'And what happened to all my clever plans yesterday, my love?' He shook his head. Bewildered. Searching her face for the answers.

'Yesterday?' She said it carefully.

'I was full of plans but nervous like a boy.' He sighed. Disgusted with himself. 'Later I wondered if I'd scared you with my serious face because I wanted you to say yes to what I asked you so badly.'

She remembered. 'Yes, you did. Scare me.' She nodded. It had scared her that he didn't care about her at all. Not one bit. But maybe that wasn't true? But she still didn't fully understand him. 'You wanted me to work for you so badly?'

'No. Yes. I am doing it again. I just wanted you to listen to my plans for our future. And part of that could be work, but most of it is you and I together. But it was a shambles.'

She couldn't deny it. It had been.

He smiled ruefully. 'And here was me with a picnic basket in the boot and a trip planned to the Park Güell to ask permission to court you slowly.'

She blinked. 'I beg your pardon?'

'We will do it all again and this time it will

work.' He shook her hands. 'If only you do not climb aboard that plane this afternoon.'

Cleo's mind raced as she pieced everything together. He'd been nervous, not aloof. Scared, not arrogant. Afraid she'd say no. Afraid she didn't want him. Not asking about work. Or moving in with Sofia. But about the possibility of a future. With him. Together. Her confident, passionate, sometimes arrogant Felipe was a mess because of her? He'd been adorably nervous and had made a mess of it all.

Had she made him nervous because he'd cared so much that she agree to his plans? That's what he'd said.

'And you were so hard and unbending, my love. So angry and determined to leave,' he said.

Yes, she had been that. Looking back. Firmly in protection mode. 'You offered me a job.'

He dropped her hands and lifted them to his face. 'My last resort to keep you here until I could move mountains and seduce you.'

She sat back. A small smile finally played around her lips. Now she recognised him. Here was her passionate flamenco dancer. 'So your plans are to seduce me?'

He nodded. Decisively. 'Absolutely, but again my grandmother would haunt me if that was all. No, my love. My plans are to make you my wife and live with you to the end of our days, teaching you again and again how much I love you.'

And he had her.

Right there. That was all he needed to say.

'Dear Felipe.' Though there was a touch of exasperation in her tone. 'A little straight talking would have helped you yesterday. Do you know why I think straight talking would have worked?'

'Tell me.'

'Because…' She swallowed. She'd known herself, had thought it, cried over it, but had never said the words, and would have to admit it out loud for the first time. 'I love you. Have loved you from the first moment I saw you in that cantina.' She leaned her head into him and tapped his chest with her finger. 'You are so hot.'

'I know,' he said with an arrogant lift of his brow, and she laughed.

But the laughter died when he pulled her close, slid his arms around her waist and lifted her onto his lap. Thank goodness Carlos was blocking the view.

He rested his forehead against hers. 'I adore you, and thank heaven for the night I found you, my beautiful Cleo.'

He looked down at her, their faces close together. Said softly, 'So, when we go for a picnic, and I bring more roses, and we walk in the park, will you listen to my reasons why you should spend your life with me?'

'Yes, I will listen, my passionate flamenco dancer.'

And then he kissed her, his relieved sigh deep and heartfelt as he cradled her face. She closed her eyes and sank into him, her arms around his shoulders, his big hands warm and gentle.

Finally, she'd found the man she'd thought she'd lost when one dawn he'd walked away from her.

CHAPTER TWENTY-SIX

Six months later

THEIR FIRST WEDDING was held in the small chapel underneath the Sagrada Familia. Weddings below the church, where there were soaring archways, were not common. After all, it was a crypt, where Gaudi, and others, rested eternally.

Only those with a certain postcode could be married there, and luckily Felipe had the right house. The architecture rose in stunning archways, a circular room with a flower of small chapels and the pulpit in the centre. Light streamed in through careful structures in the walls.

Felipe's old nanny beamed and quivered with excitement from the front pew next to Alba and Carlos. On the other side of the circular vaulted room Sofia and Isabella both looked gorgeous in pink and smiled at him.

Felipe stood tall at the altar with his cousin Diego next to him. Later there would be another wedding in the grand cathedral and the enormous reception would be held in the town hall. But Felipe had wanted this tiny, intimate gathering first, in the place that had been so special to him for so many reasons.

And now she came.

The music began and the tiny congregation turned. Beside him Diego stirred as his Jen appeared at the door in palest pink.

But Felipe had eyes only for the woman behind the bridesmaid. His bride. His Cleopatra. His queen.

And she looked every inch the queen with her head held high as she walked slowly but confidently towards him. His heart swelled as the music did, and her eyes met his. Such love shone out at him. He adored her.

He could do nothing else for he had never been so happy and hopeful for the future with his beautiful Cleo coming to stand by his side. To be his wife. His love.

And tonight, after the second wedding and the main reception, Felipe had a surprise for her. Tonight he would teach her the first steps of his dance so that for ever, together, they would dance as one. Then he would carry her to his bed and love her with all the joy in his soul.

* * * * *

If you enjoyed this story, check out these other great reads from Fiona McArthur

The Midwife's Secret Child
Healed by the Midwife's Kiss
A Month to Marry the Midwife
Midwife's Christmas Proposal

All available now!